TRAIL TO SEDALIA

TRAIL TO SEDALIA

by

Kirk Ford

Dales Large Print Books
Long Preston, North Yorkshire,
BD23 4ND, England.

British Library Cataloguing in Publication Data.

Ford, Kirk
    Trail to Sedalia.

    A catalogue record of this book is
    available from the British Library

    ISBN   978-1-84262-823-2 pbk

First published in Great Britain 1967 by Robert Hale Limited

Published in Large Print 2011 by arrangement with
Mr W. D. Spence

Dales Large Print is an imprint of Library Magna Books Ltd.

Printed and bound in Great Britain by
T.J. (International) Ltd., Cornwall, PL28 8RW

CHAPTER ONE

Jed Masters eased himself in the saddle as his horse moved slowly but steadily down the long gentle slope of thin grassland. There was relief in his tired body at the sight of Crystal City, shimmering in the haze of the hot Texas afternoon, on the flat plain some four miles ahead.

Soon he would be enjoying a cool beer with his boyhood friend Matt Gort; keeping an appointment made a year ago when Matt had persuaded him to ride the cattle drive north through Texas to the Kansas railhead. Matt had built up a reputation as a trail driver, and whilst Jed had been ramrod to a couple of outfits up the Chisholm Trail he had never worked the Sedalia Trail on which Matt had become noted.

Crystal City was sleepy under the heat of the afternoon and no one stirred on the main street as Jed entered the small town. Cowboys lolled in the shade of the sidewalk covering, casting casual, curious glances at the man who was foolish enough to ride in this heat.

They saw a broad-shouldered man, tall in the saddle. In spite of his covering of light-brown shirt and brown jeans tucked neatly into the top of short, black riding boots they could see there was no waste fat on the powerful frame. His square jaw spoke of determination and the deep-brown tan indicated a life spent in the open. There was the dust of a long trail over horse and rider moving easily along the street.

Jed's keen brown eyes travelled over the false-fronted buildings ahead. He picked out the livery stable and, with his first thought for the comfort of his horse, he turned the powerful black towards the stable. The double-doors were open and Jed rode inside before dismounting. A figure stirred from a stool beside the wall and shuffled towards Jed.

'Good day, young fella,' greeted the small bearded man, his wrinkled face mustering a smile for the new arrival. 'Wrong time of day to be ridin'.'

Jed returned the smile. 'Sure is,' he agreed, 'but I wanted to make Crystal City this afternoon.'

'In fer the cattle drives?' queried the stable-man.

'Yes,' Jed nodded. 'I'm signed-up with Matt Gort, know where I'm likely to find him?'

The old man ignored the question as if he had not heard it. 'Want your horse lookin' after?'

'Yes,' returned Jed, puzzled by the quick switch of the conversation and the apparent coolness which had supplanted the warm friendliness of the old man. Jed sensed there was something not quite right; the change seemed to come with the mention of Matt's name. Jed was about to pursue the subject, but thought better of it, besides he could mention it to Matt when he saw him.

The old man was leading the horse away. 'Mighty fine animal,' he commented.

Jed smiled, hiding his curiosity. 'Sure is, look well after him.' He handed the man a dollar and left the livery stable. He paused outside the door, glanced up and down the street and then strolled slowly along the sidewalk in the direction of the saloon.

Pushing through the batwings he paused and surveyed the room which was crowded with cowboys gathering in Crystal City to find jobs with the various outfits which would be driving cattle north. There was no sign of Matt Gort and Jed strolled across the room to the mahogany counter which ran the full length of one wall. Jed managed to find a space at the counter and called for a beer. When the barman brought the glass Jed put his question to him.

'Is Matt Gort around?'

The barman's glance changed to one of suspicion. He ignored the question, took the money from Jed, and with a curt 'Thanks' moved along the bar to serve another customer. Jed was taken aback by the reaction and was always aware of the glances of curiosity coming from two men beside him who had overheard the question. He began to turn to them for information but they suddenly became lost in their own conversation obviously wanting no talk with Jed. He picked up his glass of beer, turned round and, leaning back with his elbows resting on the counter, he looked around the saloon. Seeing an empty chair he pushed himself from the counter and walked over to it.

'Any one sittin' here?' he asked the two men at the table.

'Help yourself,' replied the dark-haired man.

Jed nodded his thanks and sat down. He sipped his beer whilst he studied the two men casually.

'Been in town long?' asked Jed.

'Two weeks,' came the reply. 'Most drovers have arrived in the last couple of days, we came early, got signed up with a trail drive starting ten miles from here.'

'If you've been around two weeks you must have come across Matt Gort,' said Jed.

The two men glanced sharply at each other then, pushed themselves to their feet and turned from the table. Annoyed by their manner Jed jumped up and grabbed one of them by the arm.

'What's the matter?' he snapped. 'I want to…'

'Leave it,' the man rasped testily, keeping his voice low. 'If you're a friend of Matt Gort you'd best forget him; you won't be welcome here.' He shook his arm free and the two men hurried to the bar, leaving an astonished Jed Masters staring after them.

His thoughts raced. What was wrong? Where was Matt Gort? Why did the mention of his name bring hostility? Matt was a like-able man. He had a reputation on the Sedalia Trail second to none. He was a good trail boss and Jed himself knew of his honesty and friendliness. Matt must be well known in Crystal City, having ridden this trail several times, yet the local people in the shape of the stableman and the barman had registered suspicion at the mention of Matt and now two drovers, who would surely know of his reputation, had revealed disgust. Had something happened to change Matt in the last year?

With these questions pounding in his brain Jed swung round and hurried from the saloon determined to find an answer. He paused outside the saloon but when he saw a placard nailed to the wall beside a door across the street he stepped down from the sidewalk and hurried through the dust of the road to the sheriff's office.

Jed knocked sharply at the door and strode in. He let the door swing shut behind him as he crossed to the desk behind which sat a slim man of about forty. His fair hair was beginning to thin a little. Pale blue eyes looked from deep sockets in a thin, gaunt face. There was a shifty look about them which registered immediately with Jed, and the look of surprised annoyance, at the suddenness of the intrusion was not lost on him.

'What's wrong with this town, Sheriff?' There was a touch of annoyance and anger in Jed's voice. 'I want some information an'

12

folks are reluctant to give it to me.'

'Calm down,' rapped the sheriff.

'Calm down?' stormed back Jed. 'All I ask is if anyone can tell me where I'll find Matt Gort an' I'm treated as if I had the plague.'

The sheriff stiffened in his chair. 'Matt Gort?' he said.

'Yes, Matt Gort,' repeated Jed. 'If no one else will tell me I figured you, as lawman, should not be afraid to speak.'

The sheriff's eyes narrowed as he watched Jed curiously. 'You a friend of Gort?'

'Yes,' replied Jed testily, annoyed that he was still not getting an answer to his question.

'How long you been in town?' queried the sheriff.

Jed looked exasperated but he figured he would get nowhere if he cut up too rough. 'Just a short while ago; look at me, I've still got the dust of the trail on me.'

'Been hangin' around somewhere out of town?' the lawman asked.

'If ridin' down from Missouri is hangin' around Crystal City then I have,' snapped Jed testily.

'Why did you want to see Matt Gort?'

Jed was getting annoyed at the continual quiz but he controlled his temper and

13

answered the question.

'Matt and I have been friends since we were boys. I hadn't seen him for some time until a year ago. He persuaded me to meet him here an' ride ramrod for him on this drive.' Jed snapped his words at the sheriff.

The lawman nodded; he was satisfied with Jed's answers. He leaned forward on his desk and looked hard at Jed.

'Matt Gort's in his grave,' he said slowly.

Jed's reaction was one of genuine shock and surprise. 'What!' The word came as a long escape of breath. He sat down in the chair staring incredulously at the sheriff. 'When? How?'

'Four days ago he was found shot behind the livery stable,' replied the sheriff.

'Murdered?'

'Yes.'

'Did you get the killer?'

The sheriff shook his head. 'No clues.'

'But I can't imagine Matt havin' any enemies,' protested Jed.

'This will surprise you,' went on the sheriff, 'but Gort was a different man to the one we used to know around here. Outwardly he was the same but several obnoxious crimes took place in the last fortnight – in fact since Gort rode in here, an' things pointed to him

14

as the criminal, in fact I view his killin' as revenge.'

'But why this attitude when I asked his whereabouts?' asked Jed.

'No one wanted to know him after the way he treated several women-folk around here; we may be a rough town when cowboys are gatherin' here but these men know how to treat their women – respect, Masters, respect. If you showed you were a friend of Gort they wouldn't want to know you.'

Jed's brain was reeling. He just could not believe this of his friend. There must have been some mistake. He voiced these thoughts but the sheriff shook his head. 'Queries I made seemed to indicate Gort was the criminal.'

'Impossible!' rapped Jed. 'There's more to this affair. How far did you get with tryin' to trail his killer?'

'Nowhere,' replied the sheriff. 'I told you there were no clues. People regarded the killin' as a blessing an' under those circumstances no one will talk.'

Jed looked thoughtful. He realized he could get no more out of the sheriff but there was something about this whole thing which did not ring true.

'You'd best forget the whole thing,' the

sheriff suggested cutting into Jed's thoughts. 'Ride out of here and leave the memories.'

Jed did not answer. He nodded and rose to his feet and walked slowly to the door. He felt the sheriff's eyes boring into him, and when he stepped outside on to the sidewalk it was like stepping into cleansing air after some undesirable, evil nightmare. Jed drew a deep breath. Leave town, forget the whole thing! That was one thing Jed would not do, at least not until he knew why Matt had been murdered.

CHAPTER TWO

Jed walked quickly to the hotel where he booked a room for an indefinite period. He insisted on having one which overlooked the main street, for he felt that from there he could see some of the comings and goings and be more in touch with the life of Crystal City than he could from the rear of the hotel. After retrieving his saddle bags from the livery stable he returned to the hotel to freshen up before seeking a meal at the town's only cafe.

As he was buttoning his clean shirt he strolled to the window and glanced out. He was turning away when he caught sight of two men in deep conversation on the opposite side of the street. He froze where he was, intent on watching the two men. They were glancing in the direction of the hotel and, as one of them was the sheriff, Jed got the feeling that they were talking about him. Jed realized he had no grounds for this feeling but he was a man who put his faith in hunches.

Concentrating his attention on the second man so that he would recognize him in the future, Jed saw a man of similar build to himself but somewhat slimmer. He was dark with a thin moustache which gave him a debonair look. His clothes were smart and Jed admired his neat turn out which was all black, adding to his striking appearance. Jed guessed he was a man well known and of some influence in the district.

The dark man appeared to talk earnestly as if issuing instructions then both men walked in opposite directions along the street.

The sun was lowering and some measure of coolness was settling on the Texas countryside when Jed returned to the hotel after enjoying a meal followed by a drink in the saloon. He had been in his room only a few minutes when there was a knock on the door. Surprised that someone should be calling on him, he crossed the room and, on opening the door, saw a youngster whom he guessed was still in his teens. Instantly Jed liked the frank open face and the wide eyes in which, at the moment was a hint of troubled concern.

The youngster hesitated a moment when he saw Jed then blurted out, 'Are you Jed Masters?'

'That's right,' answered Jed.

The caller glanced anxiously along the corridor. 'Can I come in?' he asked.

'Sure,' said Jed, stepping to one side, his curiosity roused by this youngster who had sought him out. As he closed the door behind him Jed smiled warmly to put the newcomer at his ease. 'I reckon you'd better introduce yourself before you tell me what you want with me.'

The youngster grinned shyly. 'Wes Hunter,' he replied.

'All right, Wes, sit down.' Wes did as he was told. 'Now then,' went on Jed, 'how come you know me and knew where to find me?'

'Matt Gort told me about you an' I've been waitin' for you comin',' replied Wes.

'Matt!' Jed gasped with surprise. So much seemed to be revolving around his old friend.

'When Matt arrived here over two weeks ago he immediately signed me on fer the drive to look after the remuda. He talked a lot about you; he sure was lookin' forward to havin' you with him. Then there was all the trouble and Matt's murder. After that happened I figured I'd hang on until you came.'

An excitement had seized Jed. Here was someone who had been connected with

Matt since his arrival in Crystal City, some-one who might be able to shed some light on what had happened.

'I'm glad you did,' said Jed. 'Now, start at the beginning and tell me what happened.'

Wes paused for a moment as if collecting his thoughts. 'Several women were attacked and Matt was blamed for it. He didn't do it, I'll swear he didn't, Mister Masters.' His voice rose with his protestations of inno-cence.

'All right, Wes,' put in Jed quickly. 'Keep your voice down. I don't think Matt would do such a thing.'

'He wouldn't, Mister Masters, he wouldn't.' There was a touch of agony in the youngster's voice, and Jed began to realize the torment Wes must have gone through, seemingly without a friend in town to turn to, waiting anxiously for his arrival.

'All right, Wes. Drop the Mister, Jed's the name. Now then, how did Matt come to be accused of such a thing?'

'Four attacks took place. The town was buzzing with talk about them. The first two were by someone unknown, the attacker was not recognized but after the last two, which happened on the same night, Matt was identified,' Wes explained.

Jed nodded thoughtfully. 'Who were the ladies attacked?' he queried.

'The first two live at the west end of town, the other two were saloon girls,' replied Wes.

'So it was the saloon girls who identified Matt,' mused Jed.

'Sure,' confirmed Wes. 'An' if it means anythin', Blackie Fitch, who is very friendly with one of them, was questioned a lot by the sheriff after Matt was killed but he had an alibi.'

'Who is this Blackie Fitch?' asked Jed.

'Rides for Carl Lunt, owner of the Running W spread, west of town,' answered Wes.

'What had Matt to say when he was accused?' asked Jed.

'Denied it. Said he was in the hotel but couldn't prove it,' replied Wes.

'What about the hotel clerk?' queried Jed.

'He was questioned but admitted it would have been possible for Matt to slip out of the hotel without him knowin',' replied Wes.

'So things were stacked against Matt once these saloon girls named him,' mused Jed.

Wes nodded. 'Don't know why their word was taken against Matt's.' There was contempt in his voice as he spat the words out.

Jed looked sharply at Wes. 'Lying?' he said.

'They were about Matt, maybe lying about

the whole thing,' shot back Wes.

'You mean this was no mistaken identity but a frame-up?' There was excitement in Jed's voice. His thoughts were racing with the possibility, toying with the few facts he knew. 'The first two ladies couldn't identify the attacker, planned that way, then along come two saloon girls with similar stories an' name Matt so that he is blamed for the two attacks which actually took place.' He paused momentarily. 'Was there much probin' into Matt's death?' he asked.

'Enough to satisfy the townsfolk,' answered Wes. 'Feelin' was runnin' high, an' when Matt was found dead people thought it was good riddance so they weren't too worried if his killer went free.'

Jed nodded. 'Things add up,' he said, 'but provin' them is another matter.' Suddenly he seemed to change the subject. 'How long hev you been around here, Wes?'

''Bout six months, Jed. I'm an orphan, had to fend fer myself. I've drifted. No one took much notice of me around here, then Matt arrived. I was helpin' out at the livery stable. He said he liked the way I took care of his horse an' I persuaded him to let me look after the remuda on the drive, proved I could handle horses as well as take care of them.'

'From all you've told me you're observant; what do you make of the sheriff?' said Jed.

Wes curled his nose up. 'Don't know what it is but there's something about him I don't like.'

'Same feelin' as me,' replied Jed.

'He hangs around Carl Lunt a lot,' went on Wes.

Jed nodded. 'Know a man that fits this description?' he said and went on to describe the man he had seen talking to the sheriff.

'Sure,' replied Wes. 'That's Carl Lunt.'

Jed pursed his lips thoughtfully. 'The sheriff is around with Carl Lunt a lot, does not dig too deeply into the murder because the townsfolk are in sympathy with the murderer. Presuming Matt was framed, it was done by someone who is friendly with the saloon girls who see a lot of Blackie Fitch who rides for Lunt. It's a long shot but does it make any sense, Wes?'

'Sure,' replied Wes, 'but the puzzlin' thing is motive. I don't know why anyone would want to frame Matt.'

'Tell me more about Lunt,' pressed Jed.

'He runs the Running W, biggest outfit in these parts. Has sufficient cattle to organize his own drive to the railheads. His appearance is deceiving, he's tough, an' wouldn't expect his men to do anythin' he couldn't do. He'll ride roughshod over anyone gettin' in his way.'

Jed nodded. 'Anythin' else to tell me?' he asked.

Wes shook his head. 'I don't think so,' he replied. He looked thoughtful, trying to recall any little thing which might shed some light on the mystery. 'When this trouble blew up Matt told me not to worry, things would sort themselves out.' He paused, then added, 'There was one thing, but it happened before this trouble.'

'What was it?' pressed Jed. 'Anything might be useful if I'm to get to the bottom of this mystery.'

'Matt came to the livery stable, it would be a couple of days after he had arrived in town,' explained Wes. 'He was very angry at something and kept muttering to himself. "Try to bribe Matt Gort, I'll show them." This was before he had signed me on, before he really got to know me so I don't know any more than that.'

'Bribe?' Jed muttered. 'Why should any-one want to bribe Matt?' He looked at Wes with a smile. 'Wal, thanks a lot, Wes,' he said. 'You've certainly given me somethin' to work on. I'll look into things. Hope you can get fixed up with another drive.' He saw an expression of surprise cross Wes' face.

'But aren't you goin' to take over the drive now?' asked the youngster. It was obvious that he had assumed that Jed would automatically take over Matt's position.

'I'm not known around here,' smiled Jed. 'I've not worked the Sedalia Trail so I should think that whoever Matt was goin' to boss fer will want to find someone else. I know nothin' of Matt's set-up.'

'He was goin' to take a herd made up of cattle from the small ranchers around here,' explained Wes. 'He was waitin' until you came before hirin' a crew, he wanted your judgement as well, seein' you were goin' to be his ramrod. He had arranged a meeting with the ranchers for tomorrow an' was goin' to take you to it. That meetin' is still takin' place, Jed, but it will be to try to find a new trail boss. Matt told me this would be an important drive for these ranchers as it was essential that they got a good price for their cattle because all their money's sunk in them. If they don't they'll be broke, probably hev to sell out.' Wes was talking fast and excitedly, getting out as much as he could to try to impress Jed with the situation. 'They knew they could trust Matt, he'd get their cattle through an' git a good price fer it. You've got to take their cattle, Jed, you've got to.'

Jed laughed at the urgency in this youngster's tone. He could see that Wes had pinned a lot on going on this drive and maybe that was making him see more in the ranchers' predicament than there was.

'Wes, I can't walk into that meeting and tell the ranchers that I'm goin' to take the herd,' explained Jed. 'I like your trust in me but I reckon Matt told you more about me than he should, but I expect the men Matt was working fer hev already got other plans.' Wes looked glum. Jed stepped to him and patted him on the shoulder. 'Don't take it too hard, Wes. I'm sure someone else will give you a job on a drive, besides I couldn't go, not if I'm goin' to try to clear up the mystery surrounding Matt's death.'

Wes rose to his feet. 'I guess so,' he muttered, and walked slowly to the door.

Jed felt he should say something but he could think of nothing which was adequate enough to soothe the youngster's disappointment. 'Thanks for all your help, Wes,' he called. 'See you around.'

Wes did not answer; he opened the door and walked out. Jed shrugged his shoulders,

26

searched for a cheroot, lit it and lay down on the bed blowing a long cloud of smoke into the air. He lay staring at the ceiling turning over in his mind the information he had gained.

Unable to believe that Matt was guilty of the crimes of which he had been accused Jed worked on the assumption that he had been framed. It was rather a complicated way of going about a killing but it made certain that there would be no great outcry against the killer. The killing of such a man could be hushed up whereas the killing of the popular Matt Gort, whom Jed knew, would certainly raise a furore. Matt had to be blackened in the eyes of the people and drovers, but it was the motive which was the puzzling part. Jed turned to the reason for Matt being in Crystal City. Could this have anything to do with the killing? Certainly none of the small ranchers would kill the man they had hired and put their trust in. Was someone trying to hit at these ranchers? If so, why do it by killing Matt? They would always find another experienced trail boss. The more Jed thought abut it the further he seemed to be from the answer.

In spite of his tiring ride, Jed's sleep was continually interrupted by thoughts of his friend's death, and the following morning, as he dressed, he decided on a plan of action. For the moment he knew it would be useless to question the saloon girls or to try to get anything out of Blackie Fitch. Maybe if he knew something more about Matt's contract with the ranchers he might get on to something. It was with this in mind, after enjoying a breakfast at the cafe, that he walked to the livery-stable.

The stableman's greeting was friendly but cold. 'Want your horse?'

'Please,' said Jed and before he could put a question to the man he received his answer in the man's shout.

'Wes! Wes! Saddle the big black in the fourth stall.'

Jed saw a movement at the far end of the stable and, when he saw Wes making for the stall, Jed went forward to meet him.

'Hi, Wes,' Jed greeted with a smile.

'Hi.' There was no warmth in the word and Wes avoided Jed's eyes.

'Still sore at me?' asked Jed. Wes did not answer but set about saddling Jed's horse. Jed smiled to himself.

'I need your help, Wes,' went on Jed, his voice soft but compelling attention. 'I'm ridin' to see those ranchers; I don't know where to go; care to show me?'

Wes spun round from the horse. There was a new excited look in his eyes. 'You're goin' to be trail boss?' he cried.

'Now hold on,' protested Jed with a grin. 'I didn't say that, but I'd like to go to that meeting an' make some inquiries.'

Wes let out a whoop. Already he had visions of Jed bossing a herd northwards, and Jed, recognizing the youngster's enthusiasm, did not say any more. The noise brought the stableman hurrying to see what was the matter.

'Can you spare Wes for a short time? I'm a stranger around these parts an' I'd like him to direct me.' Jed did not give the stableman time to protest but he brought five dollars out of his pocket and handed them to the man, saying, 'Can you fix him up with a horse?'

'Sure, sure, help yourself to one of our spares, Wes,' he said taking the money from Jed.

A short while later Wes was happy in the saddle alongside Jed as they left Crystal City and headed in a south-easterly direction across the grassland. Jed admired Wes' sit of a horse and the way he handled it. Matt's judgement had been right, this youngster would be good with the remuda.

They kept to a steady pace and Wes was so obviously enjoying himself that Jed did not attempt to break the silence between them. He had taken a liking to Wes, there was something about him which attracted him. Jed could not pin it down, whether it was his frank, open expression, his enthusiasm or the fact that maybe he saw something of himself at that age in him, Jed did not know.

The ground began to rise slightly, and when they reached the top of the hill Wes pulled his horse to a halt. When Jed stopped alongside he found himself looking down on a ranch-house situated at the bottom of the slope about half-a-mile distance. It was a long, low building with corrals and stables a short distance to the right, whilst on the left of the house was another long low building which Jed judged to be the bunkhouse. Even from this distance Jed could see that everything was well cared for. Beyond the house lay a four-mile stretch of grassland which rose to another hill beyond that. A trail ran along the shallow valley and Jed saw several men turn off the trail and ride beside a line of cottonwoods along a track leading to the ranch-house.

'Looks as if we're just in time,' commented Wes. He started to put his horse forward but Jed stopped him.

'Hold on,' he said. 'Brief me before we ride down there.'

'This is the Rocking Chair ranch owned by John Brady, probably the most prosperous of the small ranchers,' explained Wes. 'It could be possible that he would survive a poor price on his cattle this trip.'

Jed nodded and watched the approaching horsemen thoughtfully. Was there a man amongst them who did not want the drive to take place? If Brady could survive had he an ulterior motive in not wanting Matt Gort to take the herd? Jed pulled himself together. He was letting his thoughts run away with him. He waited a few moments longer until he was certain the horsemen would reach the ranch before him. As they neared the house he sent his horse forward down the slope at a walking pace.

There were six horses tied to the veranda rail when Jed and Wes rode round the end of the house. When they halted and Jed swung from the saddle he saw Wes hesitating.

'Climb down, Wes, you stay right alongside me,' said Jed.

Wes jumped down eagerly, feeling six feet tall, feeling a man, a partner to Jed Masters who knew just how to handle things. Jed smiled to himself at Wes' obvious delight.

Jed stepped on to the veranda and a few moments later his knock on the door was answered by a burly man. His huge frame seemed to fill the doorway. He was large in every way and his square head seemed to squat on his broad shoulders. He looked curiously, almost challengingly, at his unexpected visitors.

'I guess you must be John Brady,' said Jed amiably. He extended his hand. 'I'm Jed Masters.' Brady closed a massive fist around Jed's hand but there was not the touch of warm friendliness in it and Jed guessed here was a man whom it was hard to get to know. 'I'm a friend of Matt Gort. I was to ride ramrod for him.' Jed felt a cold hostility at the mention of Matt's name but he did not give Brady time to comment. 'I believe he was goin' to bring me with him to this meeting. I thought I would still come, thought I might learn somethin' about his death.'

Brady stared at Jed for a few moments weighing up the attitude he should take. The mention of Matt Gort annoyed him but, when Jed talked of being Matt's ramrod, Brady saw a possible solution to his problems. He stepped to one side.

'Come in.' His voice seemed to boom from the depths of his massive chest.

Jed stepped past him followed by Wes and they found themselves in a neatly furnished hall. Brady indicated a door which was slightly ajar and, pushing it open, he led the way into the room. The buzz of conversation stopped when the door swung open, and six men turned to see the three men enter the room.

Jed's eyes moved swiftly across their faces and his immediate judgement was one of friendliness from men who were typical ranchers. At the same time he detected a concern about them as if they were in the middle of thrashing out some problem.

'Gentlemen,' called out Brady after he had closed the door. 'This is Jed Masters and I think we know Wes from our visits to the livery stable.' The men nodded a greeting, waiting for an explanation for Jed's visit. 'Jed Masters,' went on Brady, 'is an old friend of Matt Gort.'

Jed detected an immediate tension come into the room.

'What's he doin' here, John? Gort's friends are no friends of ours.'

'We don't want excuses from him. Gort let us down by his behaviour.'

The protestations at Jed's presence came thick and fast but Brady broke in with his booming voice. 'Gentlemen, gentlemen. I must also say that Masters was going to ride ramrod for Gort an' would have been at this meeting in another capacity had Gort still been alive. I suggest we hear him; maybe he can help us with our problem.'

Jed felt all eyes turn on him. Their outbursts against him stopped and Jed recognized the fact that these men regarded Brady as their leader. They would tolerate his presence so long as Brady upheld it. His mind raced. How could he help these men with their problems? Whatever it was was no concern of his. He was here for information only.

'Well, gentlemen, I really came here for your help,' said Jed. 'I don't believe Matt did those things an' I am inclined to think he was framed.'

There was a gasp of surprise from the ranchers.

'Framed?' asked one of them. 'But what on earth fer?'

'I was hopin' you might be able to shed some light on that,' replied Jed. 'Is there anyone who would like to see your shipment of cattle fail?'

A murmur ran through the group of men. Astonishment showed in their faces.

'Not that I know of,' said one man. 'If anythin' went wrong I'd be ruined.'

The others agreed with him.

'What about you, Mr Brady?' asked Jed.

'I'm shippin' cattle with my friends so why should I want to see it fail?' he rasped.

'But you would survive if things went wrong?' queried Jed.

'I could, but only just,' answered Brady, anger at this quiz filling his eyes. 'You seem well informed. What are you gettin' at?'

An angry murmur ran through the men, and words in defence of Brady sprang from their lips.

Brady smiled coldly at Jed. 'You see, my friends trust me,' he said. The tone of his voice changed and he became more earnest. 'I can assure you, Masters, that I have no reason for wantin' this drive to fail. If you think I could force my neighbours to sell their land to me then you're wrong for I would not have sufficient money to buy it from them.'

Jed believed these men and there was sincerity in Brady's voice.

'I'm sorry,' he said, 'but I had to be sure I was wrong about you.' Before anyone could add further comment Jed went on to ease the tension. 'Matt was a good friend of mine an' I want to clear his name. Some things which Wes told me raised two suspicions in my mind, one of them you dealt with, now are you sure there is no one else who would want to spoil this cattle drive?'

The men shook their heads. 'No one has threatened us in any way if that's what you mean,' replied Brady. 'I can't see who would benefit from it. Do you suspect someone?'

'I have nothin' to go on really,' replied Jed. 'The connections are very slight so I'd rather not voice them.'

Brady nodded, admiring the wisdom of Jed's thinking. He looked round his fellow ranchers. 'Wal,' he said. 'Is it worth putting our problem to Masters?'

There were some doubts in the faces of some of the men but Brady decided to follow his own inclinations.

'Masters, when Gort was killed it left us in a fix,' he went on. 'He was takin' a herd composed of our cattle north. It was essential that it got through an' we got a good price fer the cattle so we hired an experienced man. Then the trouble occurred; naturally we were inclined to blame Gort for misbehaving himself and so landing us in a jam; but, after tellin' us of your suspicions, maybe we were hasty in our judgement. Never-the-less we were left without a trail boss, an' that's our immediate problem. You were hired by Gort as his ramrod I'm askin' you to take over his job of trail boss.'

Jed saw the excitement grip Wes and he knew that the youngster had been hoping this would happen.

'But surely you can find someone else,' replied Jed. 'There must be others who…'

'We've tried,' interrupted Brady. 'But trail bosses are generally hired beforehand; they don't come here hopin' to pick up a job on speck. Matt Gort must have thought highly of you to engage you as his ramrod. I've noted on other drives he was always particular about his ramrod; that's why I'm askin' you, in the name of these other ranchers, to take over our herd.'

'But that means I'll have to leave Crystal City and I'd hoped to clear Matt's name,' said Jed. 'Besides I've had no experience of the Sedalia Trail. I'm sure you could find someone more capable than me.'

'They couldn't Jed,' burst out Wes unable to contain himself any longer. 'You've got to take over the herd, Matt would expect you to.'

'Well said, Wes,' commented Brady.

The rest of the ranchers murmured their agreement.

'We're up against it, Masters, we need someone to get that herd through. If we don't we'll all be ruined,' one of the men pressed.

'But I want to finish my inquiries here,' replied Jed.

Brady looked hard at Jed. 'If your theories about someone wanting to stop our herd gettin' through are correct, and I presume you think that's why Matt was killed, then surely you would be gettin' at that person by takin' the herd.'

Jed rubbed his chin thoughtfully. 'Thet's true,' he agreed. Jed's thoughts were racing. 'It could be that if I take over the herd it will force Matt's murderer into the open, maybe I will do better trailing north than stayin' here.' He turned to Brady. 'Right, I'll take your herd,' he said and held out his hand which Brady took in a warm, firm grip.

The other ranchers relieved that their problem had been solved, crowded round Jed, and Wes, excited at the prospects, let out a loud whoop.

CHAPTER THREE

Wes was in a happy frame of mind as they rode back to Crystal City and some of his enthusiasm seemed to spill over into Jed. Jed realized there was nothing to be gained by dwelling too much on Matt's death and he hoped that his supposition that his murderer would make a move would prove correct. Whatever he did he must keep his eyes and ears open or he may finish up like Matt.

Jed wanted to get the herd assembled and on the move as soon as possible and, when he had voiced this opinion to the ranchers, they were in full agreement. Accordingly he told them he would recruit the drovers that same afternoon and that he would like each rancher to bring his cattle to a pre-arranged meeting place the next day. Brady suggested that the most suitable place would be on the north side of Pincher Creek. Everyone agreed and, with final arrangements made, Wes and Jed left for town.

'Do you know a good cook?' called out Jed

as they neared town.

Wes grinned and nodded. 'Charlie Guthrie'll sign on. Want to see him?'

Jed nodded and laughed. 'Is there anythin' or anyone you don't know? I may as well let you run this show.'

Before reaching Crystal City Wes cut off the trail and headed for a street running parallel to Main Street. Two blocks along he turned the corner and stopped outside a small shack. He swung down from the saddle, threw his reins to Jed and ran into the shack shouting, 'Charlie!'

A few moments later he reappeared followed by a short man who had a round red face, the lower half of which was covered by a small pointed beard. He was stout but nimble on his feet. His trousers seemed big for him and his striped shirt was covered by a green vest left unbuttoned. He smiled warmly at Jed who could not imagine Charlie's face wearing anything but a smile.

'Wes tells me you want a cook for the Sedalia,' said Charlie.

'Sure do,' replied Jed.

'Wal, I'm the best you'll get around here,' replied Charlie.

'Right, then you're signed on,' said Jed. 'Be out on the north side of Pincher Creek first thing in the morning. How about a chuck wagon?'

'Got my own,' answered Charlie. 'Know my way round it. Always hev it ready this time of year.'

'Good,' said Jed. 'Fill up with stores an' charge it to John Brady's account.'

The old man nodded and watched Jed and Wes turn back to the street.

As they passed an alley two blocks further on Jed suddenly pulled his horse to a halt. A scuffle in the alley had caught his attention and he saw a cowboy, with his back to a wall, warding off the attacks of three men. He was handling himself well but Jed dropped quickly from the saddle and raced to help him. He saw one man spin backwards and sprawl into the dust under the impact of a terrific blow. The cowboy staggered sideways as one of his attackers sank a huge fist into his ribs. Then Jed was on to them. He grasped one man by the shoulder, jerked him round and drove his fist hard into his face sending him staggering backwards. The first man picked himself up from the ground and flung himself at Jed who saw him just in time to step sideways and deal the man a knock-out blow as he passed. The cowboy, who was warding off a rain of blows

41

suddenly ducked under his attacker's arms and lunged into his body bringing his fist upwards as he did so. The blow connected with the man's jaw and he staggered backwards across the alley to hit the wall and slump to the ground. The only man left in a conscious state picked himself up and, with a staggering run, made off down the alley.

The cowboy turned to face the panting Jed. 'Thanks,' he gasped and drew in gulps of air to his aching lungs. 'I'm sure grateful for your help.'

'I didn't like the odds of three to one,' replied Jed breathing heavily. 'Thought I'd better help out even though you were doin' all right. What was it all about?'

'Guess I was a bit careless in the saloon an' flashed a roll of bills,' explained the cowboy. 'They must hev followed me. My name's Wade Evans.' He held out his hand.

Jed took it. 'I'm Jed Masters, and thet's Wes Hunter,' he added nodding at Wes.

Wade raised his hand in salute and Wes grinned back.

'Guess I owe you a drink,' said Wade.

'Wal, I wouldn't say no,' grinned Jed. He turned to Wes. 'Take the horses to the livery stable,' he said. 'Get yourself fixed up with a couple for tomorrow and find me another.

Charge to John Brady's account. See you at the hotel.'

'Sure, Jed,' replied Wes and rode off in the direction of the livery stable.

'Right, now for thet drink, Wade,' said Jed. He liked the look of this tall cowboy. He was slim, almost to the point of thinness, but Jed felt power in his hands and arms. He had a pleasant, angular face and his eyes shone with a keen observance. Jed reckoned that Wade's glance had summed him up in an instant and if he could do this with all men Jed figured that Wade could be useful to him. Wade confirmed this when he commented. 'Likeable youngster that. Handles a horse well.'

They picked up their sombreros from the ground, slapped the dust from them and headed for the saloon leaving two unconscious men laid in the alley.

'What you doin' in town?' asked Jed when they had got their beer.

'Same as a lot more,' replied Wade. 'Hopin' fer a job with some trail drive. I'd hoped to ride with Matt Gort, heard a lot about him as a trail boss, but I hear he's been killed.'

'Matt Gort,' repeated Jed. 'Wal, if you can handle cattle like you handled those men

43

you've got yourself a job pushing the herd that Matt was goin' to handle.' Jed smiled at the look of surprise on Wade's face. 'I'm an old friend of Matt; I was goin' to ride ramrod fer him; got into town yesterday and found he's been murdered. Today I got the job of bossin' the herd. Want the job of ramrod?'

'Ramrod!' said Wade a little surprised. 'Sure, I'll sign on.'

'Good,' said Jed. He drained his glass and called for another beer.

'What's all this about murder?' asked Wade.

Jed told him the whole story, leaving out no detail, nor theory, for he figured he could do with some allies and he judged that in Wes and Wade he would have two of the best.

When he had finished Wade looked thoughtful for a few moments. 'It sure looks as if we might have our hands full; this is an important drive for those ranchers an' you hope it might bring a killer out into the open. You can count on me to keep my eyes open. When do we ride?'

'Tomorrow,' replied Jed and went on to discuss details. 'The first thing we want are twelve drovers, figure you can get them, Wade?'

'Sure,' came the reply. 'Leave it to me. I'll have twelve fer your approval outside the hotel in two hours.'

'Good,' said Jed. 'See you then.' He left the saloon and hurried along the sidewalk to the hotel.

When he got to his room he found Wes waiting for him.

'Everything's fixed up, Jed,' said Wes.

'Good,' replied Jed. 'Wade's goin' to be our ramrod an' he's fixing a crew at the moment. Ever handled a Colt, Wes?'

'Sure,' replied Wes. 'I've never owned one but I got fairly good.'

'Right, well I think we'll go and get you fixed up,' said Jed, and they left the hotel.

An hour later as they returned Jed warned Wes that the gun was only there for an emergency, he must never get a liking for it and must be careful how he used it. He promised to teach him the best way to draw and to let him practice on their ride north.

As he pushed open the door of his room at the hotel Jed saw a piece of paper on the floor. Instant caution came to him. His right hand moved close to his gun-butt and he glanced quickly round the room. Seeing no one there he picked up the piece of paper and unfolded it. Scrawled across the sheet

45

were the words 'One thousand dollars to forget the herd, be at Three Forks at 8 tonight.'

Jed studied the words again. There was no signature; no clue at all as to the sender. His mind was racing. Word had soon got round that he had taken over Matt's job but that was inevitable once Wade started recruiting. Whoever wanted to stop this herd was in town. It certainly looked as though there was more behind Matt's killing than there appeared on the surface. Wes had spoken of Matt muttering about a bribe, were things going to follow a similar pattern with himself? Maybe here was an opportunity to come face to face with Matt's killer. Suddenly he realized Wes was staring at him, wondering what it was that held Jed's attention. He handed the note to Wes.

He read the note quickly and there was concern in his eyes when he looked up. 'You'll not accept it,' he said anxiously.

'You don't think I'm a man like that do you?' queried Jed. Wes looked somewhat distraught at the fact that he had doubted Jed's integrity. His mumbled apology was cut short as Jed went on. 'I'll not accept but I'll be there, this meeting may lead to Matt's killer.'

Wes' eyes brightened. 'I'll come along,' he

said eagerly.

'No, this could be dangerous,' replied Jed.

'Thet's exactly why I'll come. Take Wade as well. It could be a trick to kill you. Three of us could keep a better look out than one.' Wes' talk was persuasive and Jed finally agreed to his proposition.

He got Wes to describe the country around Three Forks and they made plans accordingly.

When Jed stepped out of the hotel to meet Wade he found him already there leaning over the sidewalk rail talking to twelve men grouped in front of him on the road. Wade straightened when he heard the footsteps and turned to greet Jed.

'There's your men,' he said with a smile.

'Good work,' returned Jed.

Wade introduced each man in turn and Jed had a word with everyone. He liked the look of the crew and, after speaking to the last man, he stepped back on to the side-walk.

'I'm pleased to hev you all,' he called out. 'You've all met Wade Evans, he's ramroddin' the outfit. Wes Hunter, here, is in charge of the remuda, maybe you think he looks young but I can assure you your horses will hev the best attention. For those of you without two

47

mounts there'll be some to pick from tomorrow. We're takin' a herd of cattle for the small ranchers around here. This is an important drive for them – a lot of them hev most of their money sunk in it; so I expect your full support and loyalty. Report on the north bank of Pincher Creek first thing in the mornin'.' He turned to Wade. 'Come up to my room when you're through with them.'

Jed, followed by Wes, re-entered the hotel and they hadn't been in the room many minutes before Wade arrived.

'They look a useful bunch,' said Jed.

'They'll make out,' commented Wade.

'Wade, I've told you the whole story about Matt; when I returned to the hotel a short while ago I found this under the door.' He handed Wade the sheet of paper and waited until the ramrod had read it. 'The killer has soon got on to me. If Carl Lunt is connected with this in any way he could have had that note slipped under the door; he's in town; when I was speakin' out there I saw him across the street with Blackie Fitch.'

'What are you goin' to do about this?' asked Wade indicating the piece of paper.

Jed explained his plan and, as the evening light was fading from the Texas sky, Jed rode

48

out of Crystal City in the direction of Three Forks. A mile out of town he was joined by Wade and Wes who had left earlier in case Jed was watched leaving town.

They kept to a brisk pace following Wes' directions. About half a mile from their destination Wes pulled to a halt.

'We'd better separate here,' he said. 'You ride straight on, Jed.'

Jed nodded. 'Right,' he said. 'Be careful both of you and no gun play if we can avoid it; I've sure got a lot of questions to ask of someone.'

He kicked his horse forward and Wade and Wes left the trail on opposite sides in order to circle on to Three Forks from different directions.

Jed slowed his pace so that Wade and Wes, who would have further to travel, would reach the appointed place about the same time as he did. In a short while Jed reached a point where the trail turned and dipped into a hollow at the bottom of which he could just make out in the dim light the reason for the name of Three Forks.

Around the hollow were huge upheavals of rock forming weird shapes in the light of early night. The rocks came close to two of the trails and Jed realized the instigator of the note had chosen an ideal place. Jed suddenly felt cold in spite of the warmth of the night. He could be bushwhacked here and no one would know. He was glad he had taken Wes' advice.

Jed put his horse down the sloping trail at a walking pace. He was tense, alert for any tell-tale movement or sound. Reaching the bottom of the hollow he halted and glanced around. There was no sign of anyone. He eased himself in the saddle and waited, hoping that Wade and Wes were in advantageous positions amongst the rocks.

Close behind the trail rose a bulk of rock about ten feet high and all around it leading back up the slope was a mass of tumbled boulders. Jed cast his eyes over them; the shadows seemed to play tricks and Jed had to pull himself together to stop his imagination running wild. He turned his attention to the opposite side of the trail and as he did so he stiffened in the saddle. The sound of the hammer being drawn back on a Colt was loud in the silence.

'Freeze!' the emphasis with which the word was spoken told Jed that the speaker would stand no nonsense or disobedience. The man stepped forward. Jed felt him jerk his Colt from its holster and he heard it clatter amongst the rocks when it was thrown away. 'Step down,' came the order, 'and don't turn round.'

Jed moved out of the saddle slowly. The temptation to try to identify the unknown man was great but he knew from the tone of voice, that it would be the last thing he would do. In any case there was no need to risk anything, Wade and Wes would soon make their presence known.

'Don't expect help, we've dealt with the other two.' The voice was cold, threatening. Jed stiffened. This man knew about Wade and Wes. But how? What had happened? There was a chuckle behind him. 'You weren't smart enough Masters, we kept close watch in case you tried anythin'.' The voice changed and became full of menace. 'I'll give you a last warnin', don't take that herd or you'll be sorry!'

Jed's racing thoughts, trying to probe the identity of the man behind him, trying to memorize the voice, was suddenly erupted as the barrel of a Colt cracked viciously on the back of his head. Jed pitched forward and in his unconscious state did not feel the kicks he received in his side.

Jed stirred, some measure of consciousness returned to his brain and with it came a

51

feeling of pain. A low moan came from his lips as he tried to turn over. His side felt as if it had been trampled on and there seemed to be a hundred hammers beating in his head. His eyes flickered open, everything whirled in front of him. Gradually the spinning stopped and his eyes jerked into focus. He was face downwards, his head sideways and he saw rocks rising to a star-studded sky. Then memories flooded back to him and he almost panicked when he thought of Wade and Wes. What sort of trouble had he led them into?

He tried to push himself upwards but the exertion made his head pound and he relaxed against the ground. Jed raised his arm slowly and carefully felt the back of his head. There was a long gash on which the blood was congealing. He rubbed his sticky hand on the ground and with an effort which almost made him lose consciousness again, he turned over on to his back. He lay still for a few moments then pulled himself up into the sitting position. He held his head in his hands hoping to relieve the throbbing. Jed sat for a few minutes whilst his head gradually cleared. Aware of footsteps he looked up and saw a shadowy form approaching a little unsteadily.

'Thet you, Jed?' The voice penetrated Jed's mind relieving some of his worries.

'Wade!' he called back. As Wade dropped to his knees beside him he said, 'Thank goodness you're all right.'

'Sorry, Jed,' Wade apologized. 'Someone bushwhacked me. Never got a chance to see him. What happened with you?'

'Tell you later; let's see if we can find Wes first,' replied Jed.

Both men scrambled to their feet. Jed staggered and supported himself against a rock. Suddenly a shout from the rocks above them told them that Wes was alive. They called back and a few moments later an apologetic Wes stood before them.

'Forget it, Wes,' said Jed, now beginning to feel much better. 'We were all jumped. They took precautions in case I tried to be smart.' He went on to tell them exactly what had happened and what had been said. 'But I've no idea who it was,' he concluded, anticipating their question. 'We'd better get back to town and let the doc hev a look at us.' Another ten minutes passed before they recovered their horses and were riding towards Crystal City.

When they reached the town, Wes led them straight to Doc Lacy's. He was a friendly

53

man in his middle fifties and he soon attended to them. Fortunately he reported no damage other than bruising to Jed's side and advised him to spend the next day in bed.

The following morning Jed ignored the doctor's advice and, together with Wade and Wes, was on the north bank of Pincher Creek early. But they were not the first arrivals, for Charlie Guthrie, with a fully laden wagon, was already there. In a short while the drovers began to drift in and the dust clouds foretold the approach of cattle. Two small herds were the first to arrive and as his men took over from the cowboys Jed checked the tallies with their owners.

Wes had already taken over the spare horses and had them picketed close to the chuck wagon, a short distance from the pre-arranged assembly point for the cattle. When John Brady arrived, his men brought the largest contribution of cattle as well as a number of horses. Wade Evans immediately ordered the drovers who required a second horse to choose one, and Jed settled with Brady to take an extra six along in case of emergency. Wes was happy in his work when he took over the newly arrived horses and, before long, they were picketed beside the others.

The acceptance of cattle went on throughout the morning and into the middle afternoon until Jed had a herd of three thousand under his supervision. Throughout the day Jed had not spared himself in spite of the soreness which racked his body shouting of yesterday's experience. He rode everywhere, supervising, advising, listening, suggesting and ordering. His keen eyes missed nothing. He liked the way Wade kept on top of everything with seemingly effortless ease. Jed admired the way his ramrod handled the men who, recognizing an expert, respected his judgement and orders. Jed dealt with the ranchers as they arrived, reassuring them that he had a good outfit to handle their steers all the way to Sedalia. Wes' work with the horses, his swiftness in accommodating the drovers when they came in for a change of horse brought admiration from Jed, and throughout the day Charlie kept a constant supply of coffee and had appetizing meals ready at the appointed times.

The drovers handled the cattle skillfully as they took them over, merging them together in one big herd, settling them down and calming them as they changed hands. Dust rose everywhere under the many hooves which pounded and tore at the ground. It covered horses and riders and, in spite of the neckerchiefs pulled up over their faces it found a way into nose and throat and dried up the mouth so that Charlie's coffee was a welcome slaker of thirst.

In spite of his activity Jed never ceased to be thrilled by this part of a drive, the start of a long trek, the first work together as a team when good points and bad ones came out and were blended or discarded under the skilful handling of a good ramrod and a firm trail boss.

By the time all the cattle were in and the herd settled down it was late afternoon and Jed knew that he had a crew second to none. If all went well and there were no mishaps this should be a comparatively easy trail to Sedalia. However Jed was not fooling himself – no cattle drive was easy and, after the happenings at Three Forks, trouble could spring up anywhere, at any time.

CHAPTER FOUR

Once everything was in hand Jed rode over to Wade.

'Want to go into town tonight?' he shouted as he pulled alongside his ramrod.

Wade shook his head. 'I'm on the job now, I'll stick with it.'

Jed smiled his appreciation. 'The men hev worked hard, I reckon we can let them hev a night off. Fix it so that they can all go some time or other. You an' I an' I dare say Wes an' Charlie can take care of things here fer some time.'

'Right,' called Wade and rode off to organize the night riders.

As a result of the arrangements Jed found himself patrolling the herd on the side nearest the creek at about midnight. It was a dark but starlit night. All was quiet; there was very little movement amongst the cattle and on the far side of the herd he could hear the plaintive tones of Wade's crooning. As yet none of the drovers had returned from town but Jed knew it would not be long before some of them were riding in. Their relief would be soon taking over and Jed was looking forward to sleep. He had had a hard day and had not realized how tired he was until he began to patrol the herd.

He was relaxing in the saddle, his horse barely moving when he heard the sound. At first he thought he had imagined it but on hearing it a second time he was alert, his senses tensed for any consequences. The low moan sounded again. Jed inclined his head listening intently. It came from the creek, somewhere close at hand. He turned his horse and rode towards the edge of the creek where he pulled to a halt. The moan came again somewhere to his right. It sounded as if someone was in pain. Jed was puzzled. Who would be out there at that time of night? He had heard no one moving in the creek; maybe they had been there all day. Jed strained his eyes trying to pierce the darkness. Forms seemed to grow before his eyes but he felt certain there was someone down there. The sound came again but this time it was louder; there was no mistaking a human being.

Jed swung from the saddle and started down the slope, sending loose earth and stones rolling before him. In the dark shadow of the creek side, Jed almost fell over a figure stretched on the ground. The man was laid face downwards and Jed dropped to his knees beside him. He did not notice the two shadows which rose from the rocks close by and, before he could turn the man over, a Colt crashed down on his head sending him into oblivion as he pitched forward to the ground.

The sudden pound of horses' hoofs from the direction of the creek startled Jed's three companions who were patrolling the herd. A few cattle stirred restlessly but they were soon calmed. Wes turned his horse and rode round the herd expecting to meet Jed but when the figure approaching from the opposite direction proved to be Charlie, alarm seized him.

'Seen Jed?' he asked anxiously.

'No,' replied Charlie. 'Heard some horses in the creek.' Both turned their animals towards the creek along which the sound of the fast ridden horses was fading.

As they neared the creek they were joined by Wade who spotted Jed's horse. The empty saddle alarmed them and they swung quickly to the ground.

'Spread out and work down into the creek,' ordered Wade quietly.

The three men started down the slope and a few minutes later a shout from Charlie brought the other two quickly to him. He was kneeling beside Jed and when Wade and Wes dropped to their knees they saw Jed had taken a severe beating.

Anger swelled inside Wes. He jumped to his feet. 'I'll get after them,' he snarled. He turned, but Wade stopped him.

'Wes! Stay here.' There was authority in his voice which Wes could not ignore. 'It would be useless. They're well away now an' you'd never trail them in the dark.'

Protestations sprang from Wes' lips but they were silenced by the ramrod's harsh orders.

Charlie looked up at Wes. He could see the youngster was overwrought. 'Wade's right, son, it would be no good, besides if you're goin' through with this cattle drive you've got to learn to take orders from your ramrod.'

'Sorry, Wade,' mumbled Wes.

The two older men turned their attention to Jed.

'He's in pretty bad shape,' said Charlie. 'We'll hev to get him to the doc.'

'Charlie, you an' Wes ride back to camp and you bring the wagon; we'll hev to take him to town in that. Wes, tell some of the drovers what's happened and tell them I want some night riders with the herd as soon as possible.' The two men started off up the slope. 'Take my horse, Wes, I'll go to town with Charlie.'

Once the horses made off Wade lifted Jed in his powerful arms and staggered up the slope with him. He laid him down gently at the top and waited the arrival of the wagon. He was thankful that Jed was still alive; he could easily have suffered the same fate as Matt Gort. Wade figured this was another warning, the promised outcome of the previous threat. This would be Jed's last chance to pull out; if he persisted in going on with the cattle drive he would be eliminated. All his thoughts along these lines whilst waiting for the wagon made up Wade's mind as to the line of action he would take once he had heard the doctor's report.

Jed had shown no signs of regaining consciousness by the time Charlie arrived and the two men lifted him gently into the wagon and headed for town as quickly as possible. Only the odd light showed as they drove up the main street and the doctor's house was in darkness when they pulled up. Wade jumped down from the wagon, swung through the wide wooden gate and hurried up the path.

He knocked loudly on the door and waited a few moments before he pounded again. A few minutes later as he was knocking a third time he heard someone call from inside. When the door opened a sleepy-eyed doctor peered at him, holding a lamp high so that the light fell across Wade's face.

'What is it?' There was a note of irritation in the voice.

'One of the men you looked at the other day has been badly beaten up...'

Wade's words were cut short by a doctor who was immediately alert at the news that someone needed his attention.

'Is he with you?' asked the doctor, noticing the black bulk of the wagon beyond the railings.

'Yes.'

'Then what you waiting for, bring him in.'

Wade ran back to the wagon whilst the doctor, leaving the door open, hurried to light a lamp in the room he used as a surgery.

When Wade and Charlie carried Jed in, the doctor told them to lay Jed on the blanketed table in the centre of the room.

The doctor's face was serious as he peered at the bruised, blood-stained face. There was a deep gash on Jed's right cheek and his lips were broken. The blood had run down saturating the top part of his shirt. His eyes were puffed and the right one was beginning to blacken. The doctor's gentle hands turned Jed's head sideways and he examined the ugly gash on the back of his head. He then unfastened Jed's shirt and carefully felt his body.

When his examination was over he straightened and faced Wade and Charlie whose anxiety was clearly showing on their faces.

'He's taken a bad beating but as far as I can see there's no serious damage,' announced the doctor. 'I hope he won't be suffering too badly from concussion but he certainly will have to lie up for a couple of days.'

'We're starting a trail drive tomorrow,' said Wade.

'No question of him going,' replied the doctor.

The door opened and they turned to see a young woman standing in the doorway. 'I heard the disturbance, Pa, thought you might want some help.'

'Thanks, Carol,' replied the doctor. 'This young man's had a bad beating, I'll need plenty of hot water, swabs and bandage.'

'What can we do, Doc?' asked Wade. 'Jed

won't hev anywhere to go.'

The doctor smiled and turned to his daughter. 'Can we cope, Carol?'

The blue eyes returned the smile and then held Wade who was taken by the pretty face framed in dark hair which came to the shoulders. 'We'll look after your friend,' she said. 'We come across this problem now and again with this being a drover's town.'

'Thanks,' said Wade. 'We sure are grateful.'

'Think nothing of it, son,' said the doctor. 'Now if you'll leave, I'd like to get to work.'

'Sure,' said Wade apologetically. 'Just one more thing, will you tell Jed I'm takin' the herd out at daylight, tell him not to worry an' he can catch us up when he feels fit enough.'

The doctor nodded, and Wade and Charlie left.

The doctor and his daughter worked for the best part of an hour on Jed and it was only towards the end of that time that Jed began to show signs of returning to consciousness. His first awareness was of the smell of disinfectant and as its sharpness seemed to bite into his nostrils the muzziness in his head cleared and he became aware of pain. His whole body felt as if it had been beaten with huge hammers. He struggled to sit up but firm hands held him down. Where was he? What had happened? Jed's mind began to search for a reason for feeling as he did and for being with a smell of disinfectant. He recalled a moan but no more. His face felt sore and puffed and for some reason he couldn't see anything. A panic seized him. He was blind! What had happened to his eyes? He tried to raise his hands to them but someone stopped him. He was surprised by the gentleness of the hand. A woman's hand! He must be dreaming.

'It's all right, just take it easy, I'll take the bandage off.' The voice was soft and gentle.

He wasn't dreaming; it was a woman! Jed felt something removed from his eyes. He blinked and it hurt. His right eye felt enormous and it seemed to need an effort to open it. The left eye opened first but even that felt puffed up, and when the right eye opened he found himself looking through a narrow slit. The light hurt his eyes momentarily and then he saw an oval face leaning over him. The smile revealed an even row of white teeth and there was a sparkle in the blue eyes. The high cheek bones were covered with smooth, soft skin framed by silky, black hair which fell around the face. Jed's aches and pains seemed to be momentarily relieved by the sight.

'Where am I?' The words came huskily from Jed's throat.

'You're at the doctor's in Crystal City,' replied the girl. 'I'm Carol Lacy and the doctor is my father.'

Jed saw the middle aged man appear by his daughter's side. He smiled down at him.

'You were in a pretty bad way when your friends brought you in but I think we've patched you up so you'll live,' the smile turned to a grin for a moment then the doctor became serious. 'Do you feel like talking?' he said.

'Sure,' replied Jed. 'I want to know what this is all about.'

'Well, just relax and start by telling me what you can remember.'

Jed thought for a moment. So much seemed to be in a haze but gradually he recalled patrolling the herd. He told this slowly to the doctor and then he remembered the moan. This seemed to recall a flood of incidents for Jed went on quickly. 'I got off my horse, went down the slope and came across a man face downwards. I knelt down beside him and started to turn him over – that's all I remember.'

The doctor was relieved at Jed's recollections. This tied up with what he had learned from Wade and Charlie in the few words they had had when they left the house. Jed's brain was not damaged.

'Your friends were attracted by horses in the creek. They came to see you but found only your horse. They made a search and found you had been badly beaten up. Two of them brought you here and that's all I can tell you except to give you a reassurance that, with a couple of day's rest, you should be all right.'

Jed started to protest saying that there was a herd to be moved. The doctor halted his outburst.

'Wade Evans told me to tell you that he is moving the herd out at daylight. You are to ride after them when you feel fit enough.'

Jed relaxed as the doctor spoke. He was pleased Wade was using his initiative and, after what he had seen, he knew Wade could handle things. He was glad there was going to be no delay in the movement of the herd. Besides, the way he felt he knew the doctor was right.

'Pa, I think we'd better get Jed upstairs,' Carol's voice interrupted the thoughts of the attack which were starting to flood back into Jed's mind.

'Think you can make it, son?' said the doctor.

Jed nodded and as he attempted to sit up eager hands helped him in his effort. Pain jabbed through him and it was only when he swung his feet off the table that Jed noticed the bandages swathing his body. He glanced sharply at the doctor.

'I thought you said it was nothin' serious,' he said.

The doctor smiled. 'That looks worse than it is,' he answered. 'You're badly bruised and there are some nasty cuts. You're lucky to have no ribs broken.'

Jed nodded, and as his feet touched the floor he felt dizzy. He sat back against the table.

'Take it easy for a minute,' advised the doctor. 'Whoever did this to you ought to be horse-whipped. Any idea who it was?'

'No,' replied Jed. 'Never got a look at them.'

'But it must have been planned deliberately,' said Carol. 'Haven't you any idea?'

Jed smiled. 'I hev some very slender theories an' suspicions but nothin' strong enough to make me voice them at the moment. In any case the less you know about it the better. I wouldn't want either of

68

you to be involved.'

'Report it to the sheriff,' suggested Carol.

'It would only mean hangin' around an' I must get after my herd as soon as possible. I'd be obliged if neither of you said anythin' about this.'

'As you wish,' said the doctor. 'Now ·I think you should be getting to bed.'

With the help of Carol and her father, Jed made a painful journey up the stairs and he was thankful when he was between the soft, clean sheets of a comfortable bed. A few minutes later Carol brought him some soup and it was not long before Jed was asleep.

Two days later Jed felt much better but still sore. The doctor allowed him to get up and although it was much against his grain Jed let the doctor persuade him to spend a third day with them. He was pleased he did so, for after moving about, Jed realized that had he spent the day in the saddle he would have been exhausted and unfit for further travel. On the fourth day Jed insisted on leaving. He was beginning to like a woman fussing over him and it was with some regret that he said goodbye to Carol and her father and headed out of Crystal City.

CHAPTER FIVE

Jed took the ride slowly; he did not want to overdo things but as his strength returned he grew impatient of being alone and was eager to resume command of the herd. It was during the afternoon of the third day that he saw the dust cloud rising high in the heat of the day betraying the presence of the herd. As he drew nearer he could hear the bawl of the cattle and the occasional shouts of the drovers.

Topping a rise he pulled his horse to a halt, eased himself in the saddle and leaned on the saddle-horn, thrilling to the sight before him. The longhorns were strung out across the grassland in a long, twisting, heaving stream. Wade had them moving well, they were close enough to be a well-knit unit yet with sufficient room not to hamper each other. The drag men whooping up the stragglers, preventing the herd from getting too strung out were taking the brunt of the rising dust. The slight breeze was tormenting the riders on the left side of the herd with dust, and, as Jed watched, he saw the drovers, working like the good team he expected, change positions so that no one was chewing on dust all day. Only the two point men, keeping the lead steers to a steady pace did not change positions and Jed knew that Wade had already picked out the two best men in the outfit to do this exacting job.

Jed watched the sight which never failed to thrill him, for some considerable time. The whole outfit was certainly moving as a highly efficient unit. There was no sign of Charlie with his wagon nor of Wes and the remuda and Jed knew they would be some distance ahead, maybe already at the spot picked out at which to bed down the herd.

He put his horse down the slope and Wade, who had been on the look-out for Jed throughout the past forty-eight hours, saw the movement. He turned his horse and watched the lone rider through excited eyes until he was certain it was Jed, then he kicked his horse into a gallop and earth flew as he headed to meet his trail boss.

As the two men approached each other they knew that absence had strengthened their friendship and their greetings were warm and deep.

'How are you feelin'?' queried Wade as he turned his horse alongside Jed and they slowed their pace to a steady trot.

'Fine,' replied Jed. 'A bit sore yet but thet's easin'. How's the drive goin'?'

'Quiet. Couldn't be better,' replied Wade. 'Not one spot of trouble. Sure figured we would get it when we pulled out, in spite of the warnings given to you.'

'I was sure glad you didn't wait fer me,' said Jed. 'Time's precious.'

'Thet's what I figured,' answered Wade, 'an' I reckoned if we pulled out straight away someone would be mighty surprised.'

'Guess so,' agreed Jed. 'Wonder why they haven't got at the herd since.'

'Maybe the lull before the storm,' suggested Wade. 'Hear any more of Lunt?'

Jed shook his head. 'Not a thing.'

They were nearing the herd and were discussing the future, when Wade informed Jed that Wes was worrying about him, 'He's up ahead, why not ride on an' let him know you're back. I'll bring the herd in fer the night.'

Jed grinned. 'Good idea,' he called.

They kicked their horses into a long lope keeping to the right hand side of the herd. The men were glad to see their trail boss

73

and waved their greetings as he rode past. Jed acknowledged their welcome and once they had reached the point riders the two men separated and Jed rode ahead.

When Wes saw Jed approaching he left the horses which he was picketing, jumped on to his horse and with a shout at Charlie raced across the grassland to meet Jed. Jed smiled at the enthusiasm and excitement of the youngster revealed in his galloping approach. He kept up the pace until he was almost on top of Jed then he pulled the horse into a dust-stirring, sliding halt. He turned his mount alongside Jed, questions pouring from his lips. Jed silenced him and, as they rode steadily towards the chuck wagon, Jed told Wes all the news.

Charlie was equally pleased to see Jed and was soon plying him with coffee. Wes led the horses away to lavish his care and attention on them.

Jed relaxed watching the herd approach. He studied the way the drovers handled the longhorns as they circled them, quietening them down, halting them for the night stop.

'Thought we'd bed down early an' make a start before sun-up, it's cooler then. Hope that meets with your approval,' said Wade when he joined Jed.

Jed agreed, and before long hungry drovers were riding into camp, welcoming Jed and tucking into Charlie's stew. The halt soon brought sleep to tired aching bodies and it did not take the camp long to settle down for the night leaving only the night-riders patrolling the herd, looking forward to their relief so that they too could get some sleep.

Throughout the succeeding days the herd moved steadily northwards. The excitement of the start had vanished and the men settled into the routine, monotony of the hard, lonely life of the drover. Everything was going well. The men were easy to handle and, knowing their jobs, needed little cajoling from either the trail boss or the ramrod. There were troubles and set-backs but they were the small, everyday affairs which beset every cattle drive.

Jed was somewhat puzzled that there had been no further outcome of the troubles in Crystal City. After all they were openly defying the threat and warning of some unknown person. Maybe Matt's death was not connected to the cattle drive, but there were his own experiences, the attempted bribe and the beating up which seemed to indicate that it was. If anyone was prepared to go to those lengths then surely he was not going to stop once the drive had started. Jed kept alert to any possibilities but as the days passed and the hum-drum life continued these thoughts faded further in his mind.

The drive was two days from the Brazos when Pete Logan, the scout who had done an excellent job scouting the land ahead, finding bedding grounds, warning of Indian tracks and all the other jobs, which helped with the safety of the herd, rode into camp.

He imparted three pieces of news to Jed. His report on the possible crossing of the Brazos was favourable but bad weather appeared to be moving down from the north.

'...and finally,' he went on, 'there is another herd some distance to the west headin' for the crossin'.'

'Know who it is?' asked Jed.

'Haven't ridden thet far yet,' replied Pete, 'reckoned I'd check them when they get nearer.'

'When will they make the crossin'?' queried Jed, knowing that it was important for him to get his herd across first. 'They are about a day behind us,' answered Pete.

'Good,' said Jed, 'then if all goes well we should cross first. Keep your eye on thet herd, Pete; we'll try to push the herd a bit harder tomorrow an' gain a few miles.'

As the drovers bedded down for the night they eyed the darkening sky with some apprehension; they were in for their first soaking of the drive. Low cloud scudded overhead and it began to thicken, hastening the night. The cattle stirred uneasily when the rain began to lash them and they heard a distant rumble. Jed eyed the lightning in the north-eastern sky with some misgivings. Storm hit cattle were uneasy and the least thing could stampede them when they were in this state.

'Hope that lightning keeps away from us,' commented Wade. 'Figure I'll put on a couple of extra night riders.' He hurried away and in a few minutes two drovers were riding from camp to join the four men already slowly circling the herd, soothing and calming it as the rain lashed down with renewed frenzy.

The thunder rumbled nearer and disturbed tired drovers trying as best they could to snatch some sleep in readiness for tomorrow's drive. It was shortly after the first night riders had been relieved that the full fury of the storm hit the herd. Thunder crashed overhead and lightning streaked from the sky. Cattle bellowed and moaned, rose to their feet frightened by the noise. They pushed against each other sending a ripple of fright across the herd. As the thunder crashed again and again Jed was on his feet calling to some of his men to help the night riders calm the herd.

Before the men could carry out his orders there was a sudden disturbance on the west side of the herd. Steers bellowed loudly with fright, turned and pushed and shoved against each other, trying to get out of the way of something which terrorized them. Lightning forked downwards seeming to strike at the very herd itself. It was the final touch to the herd through which was already running the terror of the unknown. Steer crashed against steer, their horns ripping into flesh. The movement went right through the herd until the steers on the far side turned, gave way and ran. The rider directly in their path whooped and shouted trying in vain to stop the rush, then realizing the danger he was in, turned and ran with the cattle hoping his cow-pony would keep its feet. One slip and he would be pounded to death beneath the earth-tearing hoofs.

Jed stared at the upheaval, thrown into sharp relief by the flashes of lightning. As the herd turned and ran he raced for his horse. Wes was already throwing a saddle on it and the other drovers were saddling up with all possible speed. As soon as a man was in the saddle he was heading for the herd at a dead run. Jed and Wade found themselves alongside each other their powerful animals stretched across the grassland. They were soaked before they had gone far but they did not notice the wetting in their anxiety for the cattle.

Drovers raced after the herd and drew their horses close alongside the frightened cattle, trying to keep them in a close compact mass and prevent them splitting into groups. But already steers were breaking away from the main body. As the lightning lit up the scene Jed saw three riders close to the front of the herd. He urged his horse onward, and, ignoring the cattle close to him, gradually moved towards the front of the herd. The three men were trying in vain to turn the lead steers and Jed threw his effort to their help. For a moment, he thought some of the steers were going to give way to the pressure thrown on them by the riders, but suddenly several of them twisted, avoided the horsemen and split away across the prairie.

One of them turned his horse sharply to

79

chase them but, on the surface made greasy by the rain, his horse slipped and he was flung from the saddle as the animal went down. The man was on his feet in an instant looking for some escape from the cattle splitting away from the main body. Jed saw the man silhouetted in the white light of a vivid flash and turned his horse sharply. He felt the hoofs slip, for a moment he thought he was going down, but then the animal found a grip and Jed was racing towards the drover. The man saw him coming and, realizing Jed's intention, braced himself for the pick-up. Jed slowed as he neared the man and brought his horse almost to a halt alongside him. Jed leaned from the saddle, gripped one of the man's arms as he grasped at the saddle and heaved, helping the man's upward motion. The drover swung behind Jed who put his horse into a gallop as steers pounded alongside them.

Jed ran with the small group of cattle for a short distance before he was able to slip away from them. As he stopped the horse and turned to survey the scene he guessed the worst had happened. The storm, moving south, still lit up the grassland with its flashes of lightning but the thunder was not as bad as it moved further away.

'Thanks, Boss,' panted the man behind him.

Jed slapped the man's leg in reassuring acknowledgement. His eyes pierced the darkness and, with every flash silhouetting the running cattle and riders, Jed saw the drovers had not been able to bring the stampeding herd under any sort of control. It was split into groups of steers pounding across the grassland in different directions. Jed realized there was nothing they could do but let the animals run themselves out, and then tomorrow start the laborious search of seeking out the steers and bringing them back.

He stabbed his horse forward and rode slowly in the direction of the camp. They were the first to arrive and were thankful for the hot coffee which Charlie had ready.

A short while later drovers began to drift in and when Wade rode in Jed felt happier.

'We managed to keep a bunch of cattle together and when the split occurred we were able to turn them in a circle an' let them run themselves out,' said Wade.

'How many men with them now?' queried Jed.

'Four,' answered Wade.

'Then no one has been hurt, thank goodness,' said Jed. He took his ramrod to one side.

'Any idea what caused the stampede?' asked Jed.

Wade looked at Jed in surprise. 'The storm,' he replied. 'Hev you some other idea?'

'The cattle were restive naturally, but I didn't think they were on the point of stampeding. In all probability it would hev come but I was gettin' the men out an' I think we could hev prevented it. Some disturbance panicked them sooner than I expected.'

'The storm was bad,' said Wade. 'Sure you're not imagining it?'

'I suppose I could be,' answered Jed. 'We'll hev a word with the men who were on night watch at thet time.'

The rain was easing when Wade sought out the four men. Jed's questioning revealed nothing; they were all of the opinion that the storm had caused the stampede. When Jed mentioned the disturbance Shorty Jones who had been riding on that side of the herd admitted the stampede had started there but had put it down to a particularly bad flash of lightning.

The drovers were relieved when the rain had ceased. They got what little rest they could but because of the uncomfortable conditions everyone was up and about long before first light. Charlie arranged an early breakfast so that by the time the sun came above the horizon every man was in the saddle searching for cattle. They searched far and wide across the grassland finding longhorns in hollows, creeks and gullys or just drifting on the open stretches. Drovers cajoled them up the slopes and across the prairie, hazing them back towards the camp. Gradually throughout the day the herd grew until it was almost the original size. Some cattle had been lost, run too far or had been trampled under the feet of the rest of the stampeding longhorns.

It was a hard day for both men and horses in the heat of the sun and Jed's hopes of being able to cover some miles towards the Brazo in order to keep the advantage over the other herd gradually vanished. It would be expecting too much to ask the men to try a night drive. By tomorrow the day's advantage which they held would be gone. All Jed could hope for was to outrun their rivals in a dash for the river.

CHAPTER SIX

Jed had the herd on the move early the next morning and informed the drag men to press the herd hard. An unrelenting pace was kept up which meant a great strain on both men and horses but by the time they bedded down Jed was well satisfied that they would reach the river crossing about mid-afternoon the next day. He felt that at the pace they had been going that they would have regained some measure of their advantage. He had waited anxiously all day for some report from Pete Logan but he did not show up.

The following morning the herd was moving steadily towards the Brazo when Jed and Wade spotted Pete coming in at a fast gallop and immediately turned their horses to meet him. There seemed to be some urgency about his ride and Jed was feeling somewhat apprehensive when the three men pulled to a halt.

'How far off are they?' called Jed anxiously.

'It's a neck and neck race,' answered Pete steadying his restless horse. 'They must know about us because they are starting to push hard.'

'Right, we'll give them a run for their money,' rapped Jed rising to the challenge.

He started to turn his horse but was halted by Pete. 'One other piece of news, boss,' he said. 'Thet's Carl Lunt's herd!'

'What!' Jed exchanged glances with Wade. 'Maybe that stampede was deliberate after all, Wade,' he said. 'Deliberate to delay us so Lunt could catch up.'

'But how could Lunt hev organized it?' queried Wade doubtfully.

'I don't know,' replied Jed, 'but if Lunt gets to the crossin' first we'll be held up again. He'll stay ahead all the way into Sedalia an' it will also give more herds time to be there ahead of us. A flush of cattle and the price could fall. C'm on let's git that herd movin' fast. Keep a check on Lunt, Pete.' He kicked his horse into a gallop and with Wade beside him raced for the herd.

Soon every drover knew the seriousness of the situation and put every effort into out running Carl Lunt's herd. A man was dispatched to contact Charlie and Wes, who were some distance ahead, with the news that they were to push ahead and cross the Brazos as soon as possible.

The point men urged the lead steers onwards and with the drag man exerting pressure from the back, the herd went into a run, but it was a well controlled run. Nothing must get out of hand at this stage or there would be chaos. The drovers kept the herd loose but compact. Wade and Jed were everywhere, never sparing themselves. They advised and ordered, shouted and yelled and saw a response come from the men which seemed to spill over into both horses and cattle.

Jed was pleased when the drover returned to report that Charlie and Wes were safely across the Brazos. It looked as if they might be winning the race but Jed kept a watchful eye on the dust-cloud marking the progress of Lunt's herd. They seemed to draw ahead and then Jed doubted his own judgement. It was a great fillip to everyone when Pete rode in to say that Lunt was behind and they were winning the race but shortly afterwards when he reappeared, to report that seven of Lunt's men had ridden ahead and were in the path of Jed's herd, Jed knew they would have a tough fight on their hands. He realized that Lunt must know he was outrun and was prepared to make a deliberate attempt to try to hold up Jed's progress.

Jed did not falter but kept the herd moving at this winning pace. He told Pete to stay with him and then sought out Wade to whom he broke the news.

Wade's face was grim. 'Looks like a gun battle,' he commented.

Jed nodded. 'We three will move up front with the point men.'

They spurred their horses and Wade galloped ahead, swung across the front of the herd to warn the point man on the right of the danger. Whilst Jed and Pete stayed with the man on the left. Jed glanced round to check the herd and was pleased to find it moving at a brisk pace whilst being held compact by his men. At all costs they must keep the steers moving forward. Lunt's men would make every effort to turn the leaders and, if they succeeded the whole herd would follow and, turned from the river would enable Lunt to make the crossing first.

The five men were tensed in the saddles, their eyes straining for the first glimpse of Lunt's men. Jed saw them first, strung out in a line across their path about a mile from the river. They were mounted, guns drawn, seven grim, determined figures menacing the drive to Sedalia, menacing the future of several small ranchers way back in Crystal City.

Jed glanced at the men beside him, their lips were drawn in a tight line, Pete's eyes narrow in annoyance, the point man's head high with defiance. Jed looked beyond them and saw Wade glance in their direction. He waved encouragement which Wade acknowledged. After flexing the fingers of his right hand, Jed drew his Colt and spurred his horse to widen the distance between himself and the herd. His men followed suit. For a while time seemed to hang still, the distance between the rival parties did not seem to lessen then suddenly it had flashed away and Colts roared.

The seven men held their horses steady as they stirred uneasily with the herd pounding towards them. They held their fire until the last possible moment then poured a volley of shots at the advancing longhorns. Shocked by the unexpected the lead steers faltered but, pushed on by the cattle behind them, kept up their forward run. Lunt's men spurred their horses and split as Jed's men returned their fire. Jed realized they were going to concentrate on the cattle, five men rode directly at the herd whilst the other two moved to the outside of the herd to hinder the drovers. Jed wheeled his horse across the herd and saw Wade do the same. His Colt roared as a cowboy bore down upon him. The man wheeled his horse and was past, pouring lead at the lead steers. Everything seemed to happen in a rush. One of the steers went down, the others seemed to hesitate, bellow with fright but, finding no easing of the pressure behind them, rushed on. As he wheeled his horse sharply Jed saw a cowboy fall from his horse and was aware of Wade galloping towards the advancing herd his Colt blazing at four of Lunt's men who were turning in front of the herd trying to force the lead steers to the right. Pete was coming in at a full gallop followed by the point man and beyond the herd Jed saw a riderless horse galloping away. A rider crossed in front of him and Jed squeezed the trigger. The man stiffened in the saddle as if a great hand had struck him in the side then he tumbled to the ground in the path of the pounding longhorns. Jed had no time to think of the man for he was wheeling his horse for his own safety. The powerful animal dug in his hoofs and, with muscles straining, moved away from the cattle. Jed saw two more animals crash to the ground and the herd seemed to split a little, hesitate and then come back in one pounding mass moving to the right. The remaining four Lunt's men were succeeding. The longhorns were frightened, yielding to pressure, seeking some way to avoid the terror of flying bullets and yelling men. Jed spurred his horse in an endeavour to get across the herd. A figure rode down on him and he felt a bullet whine close to his ear. Jed kept his horse at full stretch and saw Wade and his point man a little ahead of him, obviously with the same idea of getting to the side of the herd to exert pressure to bring it back on the straight run. As he swung round the point Jed saw that some of his men, who had been riding along to the side of the herd, had realized the danger and were moving up.

It seemed a lifetime to Jed before their exertions bore results and the longhorns were eased back on to their former run. It was only then that he realized that the pressure of Lunt's men on the front of the herd had been eased by Pete Logan and his point man who had followed across the front of the herd but held back to harass the men with blazing Colts. He eased the speed of his horse, saw the would-be destroyers riding away at full gallop in the direction of Lunt's herd. They had won; they would be first to cross the Brazos.

Jed turned his attention to the herd. It was moving too fast for his liking. Then Wade was alongside him. Jed grinned his appreciation and yelled above the thundering pound.

'We'll hev to slow them, daren't hit the river at this speed.'

Jed pulled his horse round to gallop to the rear of the herd and Wade moved quickly to the front, yelling instructions to the drovers. Jed, realizing they had not far to run to the river, kept his horse at full gallop until he swung round the back of the herd into the choking swirling dust. The drag-men, unaware that all was well up front were still pressing the longhorns hard. Jed sought them out quickly yelling to them to ease the pressure then he was swinging around the side of the herd to race back to the front. He found that Wade and his men were handling the steers skillfully, exerting influence here, easing pressure there until the steers, sensing the danger was over, began to slow their run. Feeling no urgent pressure behind them they slowed even further until, with the river in sight, they were down to a walking pace.

Jed made a swift check before the crossing. The men had changed their horses for those which were strong swimmers before Wes had left with the remuda. One man who had received a flesh wound during the attack was sent ahead to cross the river and get attention from Charlie. Once Jed was satisfied, he and Wade rode off to examine the river before committing the cattle to it. A quick survey of the crossing was all that was necessary. The current was swift but not impossible and Jed estimated that if they put the cattle into the water about a hundred and fifty yards to the left they would be carried by the current to the outlet on the opposite side.

'Charlie must hev had to detour,' said Wade, 'there's some swimming water there.'

Jed nodded. 'Looks as if Wes has made it all right.' He turned his horse. 'I'll take four men to keep them movin' out on the other side, the narrow exit could cause a bit of trouble.'

They galloped back to the herd and, after Jed had picked out four men, they set the steers at the water. The slope to the river was gentle and they had little difficulty in persuading the lead steers to enter the moving water. Deeper and deeper they waded until about a third of the way across they had to swim. Jed and his four men kept on the down-stream side of the longhorns, urging and persuading them onwards. They battled against the current, being carried downstream as they moved across. For a few moments Jed was anxious, in case his judgement of the entry point had been wrong, but when a steer found the river-bed beneath its feet, close to the narrow passageway from the river, Jed was relieved. The other lead steers were close behind and Jed rode out on to the river bank to survey the scene behind him.

With the lead steers taking kindly to the water Wade had not a great deal of trouble in persuading the other cattle to follow. Jed saw a long line of longhorns strung out in an arc across the river. As steers moved past him he realized that if too many were allowed into the water they would press too hard and the exit from the river would become congested, resulting in some losses.

He issued orders to his four men quickly telling them to allow the cattle to drift once they reached the bank. Whilst two of them concentrated on urging the cattle away from the river bank the other two worked them out of the water, Jed put his horse back into the river, recrossed it and, after instructing Wade about letting the cattle into the water, he returned to help on the other side of the river. Throughout the whole operation Jed did not spare himself, he was in and out of the water all the time, shouting instructions, urging steers onwards, and supervising the whole transference of the herd across the Brazos. Jed was thankful when the last steer was across and he counted himself lucky that not one animal had been lost.

Pete, who had ridden off, after the first steers were across, to find a bed ground, returned to report that there was a suitable one three miles further on. Charlie was already on his way there and Wes was holding the remuda about a mile away in case anyone wanted a change of horses.

The cattle were scattered over a wide area and Jed issued instructions for the men to haze them into the bed ground. He then recrossed the river and rode until Carl Lunt's herd came in sight. He halted his horse on a rise and studied it carefully. Satisfied, that from all appearances, Lunt was not going to attempt to cross the Brazos that day, Jed returned to find the cattle being reassembled, and before long the men were enjoying the few reliefs of a night camp. Jed was satisfied that they could now keep ahead of Lunt all the way into Sedalia unless something unforeseen occurred.

CHAPTER SEVEN

There followed days of monotonous travel, the routine, boring life of a trail drive pressing north for the railheads. Jed detailed a man to hang back for a few days to keep an eye on Lunt. The daily reports showed no sign of retaliation on Lunt's part.

The days dragged on with Lunt still observing the code of the trail and not attempting to pass Jed's herd which kept in a travelling condition. As the days passed it became as if Lunt had never created any trouble and the threat of this rancher faded somewhat in Jed's mind.

Then came Sulphur Springs.

Beyond this town was a long stretch of bad trail and it was essential for a drive to get well supplied before moving into this section of the country. Jed had told Pete to find a good bedding ground to the east of the town and all the drovers were relieved when he reported one not far away. Now there would be an easing up for a day and they knew their trail-boss would see to it that they all got a break in town.

The following morning Jed accompanied Charlie into Sulphur Springs and took Wes along with him. Sulphur Springs was only a small place, little more than a trading place, making most of its money when the herds were trailing north but here the drovers could find relief from the drive, could find beer to take the place of dust, and female company as a change from the long, all male days.

Jed was somewhat surprised to find a wagon outside the store but did not pay a great deal of attention to it. He told Wes to help Charlie load the wagon whilst he went in search of a beer. He had barely tasted the cool drink when Wes hurried into the bar.

'There's trouble at the store, Jed,' he panted. 'Lunt's over there.'

'What!' Jed was astounded. He ignored the rest of his beer and hurried from the saloon with Wes beside him. He crossed the dusty roadway and swung into the store. 'What's wrong, Charlie?' he demanded eyeing the black clad man who leaned against the counter puffing a cheroot. The storekeeper looked a little bewildered and frightened.

'There's nothin' to buy, Jed,' answered Charlie.

'What!' Jed was amazed and looked at the storekeeper for some explanation. The small, bald man shook his head and cast Lunt an apprehensive glance. Jed looked at the rancher who gave him a smile of one who knows he holds the upper hand.

''Fraid it's true,' said Lunt smoothly. 'I don't think we've had the pleasure of meeting. I believe you're Jed Masters.'

'Sure,' snapped Jed irritably. 'I know who you are, maybe we hevn't met but our paths hev crossed.' Lunt grinned. 'Now explain yourself,' demanded Jed.

'It's simple,' replied Lunt calmly. 'I've bought the lot.'

Jed stared incredulously at the dark-featured man. He could hardly believe anyone could buy everything in the store.

'But you can't. I need provisions, you don't want it all,' Jed protested.

'I can an' I hev,' rapped back Lunt.

Jed looked at the storekeeper. 'Is this true?' he asked.

The man nodded. Lunt's grin broadened. He threw his cheroot on the floor and ground it out with his heel.

'It's true enough, Masters,' he said.

'But I'm low on food,' said Jed. 'I can't cross the next stretch without stockin' up.'

'Then you're goin' to have to wait until the next supplies arrive,' said Lunt smoothly. 'About a week the storeman tells me. You won't be in travel condition, Masters, so you'll hev to let me pass.'

There was a cold determination, coupled with satisfaction, in his voice.

Jed's brain was racing. This was another of Lunt's schemes to delay the herd so that by the time it got to Sedalia prices would be at a low level, and such prices meant ruination for the small ranchers.

In a flash Jed's gun had left its holster and was covering Lunt menacingly.

'You're not gettin' away with this one Lunt!' he snapped. 'You've tried all sorts to stop the herd gettin' through, I don't know why but...'

'What're you talkin' about?' cut in Lunt, feigning incredulity.

'You know,' rapped Jed testily. 'Matt Gort's murder, the warnin' I received an' the beatin' up I got because I didn' take heed. Stampede an' the attempt to stop us crossin' the Brazos, an' now this.'

Lunt did not move from his position. There was a look of contemptuous disbelief on his face and Jed realized he would not draw the man into making a slip of admission.

'I don't know what you're talkin' about, Masters,' he drawled. 'I won't deny my men tried to stop you crossin' the Brazos so they could get there first but it wasn't on my authority; I've only joined the herd recently.'

'What about this?' snapped Jed, irritated that Lunt had an explanation. 'Don't tell me this isn't your doin'.'

'I won't deny thet,' smiled Lunt smoothly. 'But then we're movin' into a bad stretch an' I want all the stores I can get. I'm payin' for them so you can't say that's illegal.'

'Your method's fair an' square,' admitted Jed, 'but your intention isn't. I'm havin' the stores I require so back off an' let my man get what I want.'

Lunt hesitated and straightened. Jed was a little mystified that there wasn't a sign of anger in the man. Suddenly a Colt roared somewhere just behind Jed. Instinctively he started to move but he stopped himself, otherwise his vigilance of Lunt might have been impaired and Lunt might have been able to draw on him. He saw Lunt's expression change. The casual almost nonchalant attitude, even though covered by a Colt, disappeared and was replaced by one of annoyance which turned to anger.

Wes stepped alongside Jed and Jed noticed

the Colt in Wes' hand.

'His hombre from his wagon came in an' tried to get you from behind,' said Wes. There was a slight tremor in his voice after the shock of his first killing.

'Thanks,' said Jed. 'Don't let it worry you – it was necessary – he would hev killed me if you hadn't got him. Now help Charlie. Charlie', he called over his shoulder, 'load up with what you want.'

Charlie stepped forward and he and Wes loaded the wagon with all the supplies for the next long stretch of the drive. Throughout the procedure Carl Lunt watched without speaking. He was fuming at the way his scheme had failed. He should have got here sooner and been clear of the town before Masters arrived. He searched for a way to turn the situation to his advantage but he found none.

When Charlie and Wes had finished, Jed told Wes to disarm Lunt. He then ordered Charlie and Wes to leave town. When he heard the wagon was under way Jed backed slowly to the door where he stopped.

'Lunt,' he said, emphasizing his words. 'Keep clear of me; this herd is goin' through; don't try to stop it or you'll answer to me.'

Before Lunt could reply Jed stepped out of

the store. Three steps took him to his horse. He unhitched it from the rail and swung into the saddle almost with the same movement and galloped after the wagon which was rumbling out of Sulphur Springs. Had he known that Carl Lunt, annoyed and frustrated by what had happened, was waiting to keep an appointment Jed would certainly not have left Sulphur Springs when he did.

They were half way back to the herd when they sighted a bunch of riders heading in their direction. A few minutes later they recognized some of their own crew and knew that Wade had organized the work so that everyone would get into town.

Wade was somewhat perturbed when he heard Jed's story of Lunt's attempt to upset their drive.

'I hope he hasn't got any more tricks up his sleeve,' he commented. 'We're facin' a rough part of the trail an' we sure don't want any trouble along it.'

'Don't see what he can do when we're on the move again,' commented Jed.

He would have had second thoughts, however if he had known that at that moment Carl Lunt was issuing instructions to a man who had just arrived in town.

The next morning, in spite of some aching heads after a night in town, the drovers were in their saddles early and the herd was on the move before sun-up. It was a wearying day, the sun burned hotter than ever and the land seemed to be dustier, the steers were sluggish as if sensing a hard drive ahead before they reached the Red River.

The drovers were glad when it was time to call a halt and after the herd had been bedded down the weary men rode into camp eager to be out of the saddle. As soon as they had finished their meal several of the men turned in but four relaxed with a pack of cards playing poker on an upturned box. Shorty Jones sauntered over to watch them and Jed was talking to Charlie beside the chuck wagon.

The game had been in progress for about ten minutes when there was a great shout and the box and the cards were sent flying across the ground. Jed spun round to see two of his men on their feet facing each other angrily.

'You're a liar,' yelled one. 'Shorty here saw you pull a card off the bottom.'

'He's the liar if thet's what he told you!' yelled back the other drover.

'How come you've been winnin' all along

if you hevn't been cheatin?' shouted the first one.

'Lucky streak,' snapped the second.

'Cheating!'

The accused drover lunged forward driving his fist into the other man's face sending him sprawling into the dust. Jed leaped forward when he saw the man on the ground clawing for his Colt his own gun flashed into his hand and he was standing over the drover menacingly.

'Leave it!' The order rapped out sharply.

The man stopped. His dark angry look flashed from Jed to the men behind him.

'Get up!' ordered Jed, and waited until the man had climbed to his feet before he spoke again. 'I don't know which of you is right an' I'm not goin' into that, but this I will say; I'll hev no gun play, on my drive, no fightin' amongst yourselves. We've plenty to think about gettin' these cattle through. I know we've had a tiring day an' no doubt you're sufferin' from the effects of your break in Sulphur Springs but that's no concern of mine – I want a full, fit crew to push cattle tomorrow so cool off an' get to bed.'

The men looked sheepishly at each other and at their trail boss. With muttered apologies they shuffled away to their bed-rolls.

Jed took one of the card-players to one side.

'Did you see what happened?' he asked.

'Nothin',' replied the drover.

'Then how did it start?' queried Jed.

'It all started when Shorty whispered something to Sam, reckon he must have claimed he'd seen Burt cheat.'

Jed nodded. 'I see,' he said. 'Thanks.'

This was the first incident they had had between the men and, whilst he felt a little perturbed about it, he put it down to the hard day. Never-the-less the incident was mentioned to Wade who said he would keep an eye on things. The ramrod, unbeknown to Jed, spoke of the incident to Wes.

'I want you to keep your eyes an' ears open for any likely trouble, Wes,' he said. 'You're around all the men a lot, seein' you handle their horses, and you can watch them without them being suspicious of you.'

'What do you expect will happen, Wade?' asked Wes.

'Don't know,' replied the ramrod. 'Jes hev that feelin' thet Carl Lunt isn't goin' to give up tryin' to stop this herd.'

'But what has thet to do with the upset over the cards?' said Wes.

'Maybe nothing',' said Wade. 'Can't see how it can really, but...' He stopped, then added. 'Doesn't matter Wes. Jest keep your eyes an' ears open.'

He left a somewhat mystified Wes who was determined to do as Wade had asked him.

The drover's life was hard under any circumstances but this part of the trail with its poor grazing and lack of water proved tough for the men riding for Jed Masters. Jed had taken precautions regarding water and had made sure Charlie had a more than ample supply on his wagon and that each man had a full canteen. As the days progressed and the sun grew hotter men were tempted to use more water. When they found the first two water-holes dry Jed began to view the situation with serious misgivings. If it was like this all the way to the Red River things were going to be bad. Jed had to make a strict rationing of the water but his big concern was for the cattle. Peter rode far in search of water-holes but every time he returned it was with a dismal report. The burning sun seemed to have sucked all the moisture out of the earth.

The men became irritable and critical. They had never been like this before and it worried Jed because, in his opinion, his crew although pushed by the wearying, trying conditions would have risen above petty feelings. It was easy in this mood for arguments and quarrels to start and, on a number of occasions, both Jed and Wade had to separate men. These feelings, coupled with the conditions, all made for a lowering of the efficiency of the drive. It was as if there was a current of unrest throughout the crew, yet neither Jed nor Wade could pin it down to anything definite. Men became careless, the tightness of the herd slackened which all helped to slow down its progress and it was essential that the pace should be kept brisk in order to reach water as soon as possible and prevent Carl Lunt from pressing them too hard.

On more than one occasion Wade had to admonish the drag men for not keeping the stragglers close in, thus allowing the main herd to slacken pace because it was not under pressure. The men riding the side of the herd allowed it to splay out and several times cattle broke away in search of water causing delay until they were recovered.

Day after day the dust rose in great clouds as the herd moved onwards. It covered both men and animals alike. Even the neckerchief pulled up over the face did not act as a preventative; the dust found its way into their throats, choking them with its dryness. It got under their clothes irritating their skin. Every man wished and longed for rain but every morning they awoke to find a clear sky and the promise of a scorching sun.

The situation worsened and the ugly seeds of suspicion were sown when it was discovered one day, only after the coffee had been made for breakfast, that the remaining water supply had been ruined by the addition of salt from Charlie's supply. Tempers ran high and everyone suspected everyone else, when the full realization of the torturous ride ahead struck home. The anger of the drovers took some quelling but finally when the noise eased Jed was able to speak.

'We're still an estimated four days travel from the Red River. I hope we'll find water before then, but we must be prepared for the worst. This means we'll hev to push the herd harder though goodness knows how the cattle will stand up to it. I want everyone's cooperation in this matter. I know there's someone amongst us has ruined the water an' put us in a tight spot. I intend to find out who it is an' when I do, Heaven help him.' Jed's voice left no doubt in the drovers' minds how hard he would be on the culprit.

'Can't some of us ride to the Red River and get water?' called Shorty Jones.

'Thet would mean sending the wagon to carry it,' replied Jed, 'an' those left behind wouldn't hev food.'

'Leave the food with the herd,' suggested another man.

'Thet means keepin' the herd here until you return,' replied Wade.

'An' I'm not doin' thet,' put in Jed. 'Carl Lunt is pressin' us hard an' if he finds this herd not travellin' he'll claim the right to pass us an' that'll put him into the market first. If I let that happen I'll be lettin' those small ranchers down.'

'We're more important than they are,' shouted Shorty. 'I say we go for water even if Lunt does pass us.'

There was a shout of agreement from some of the men. Jed exchanged glances with Wade.

'We're pushin' this herd,' yelled Jed firmly, his voice carrying unquestionable authority. 'You've all got a canteen of water an' it's up to you to make that spin out. The sooner you get the herd to the Red the better it will be for everyone.' He did not wait for an answer but went on. 'Now git movin', you're all wasting time here.'

Some of the men hesitated but seeing Jed would stand no nonsense they strode away. When the men had reached their horses Jed turned to Wade.

'We'll hev to watch them,' he said, 'an' we'll hev to keep pushin' the herd hard.' Wade nodded. 'Shorty Jones seemed to hev a lot to say,' commented Jed, 'an' he was behind that incident over the poker game way back; could he be behind the unrest which has crept in?'

'I've wondered the same,' replied Wade quietly, 'but I don't see why.'

'Maybe it's deeper than we think,' said Jed. 'C'm on we better git the herd movin'.'

The two men hurried to their horses which Wes had saddled for them.

Soon the herd was under way and throughout the day Jed and Wade were relentless in their pressure on the men. They knew they would be unpopular, as this was contrary to the way they had run the drive so far, but Jed also knew that the men would bear them no malice when they realized the necessity of the pressure. To gain a few extra miles Jed pushed the herd on after their normal stopping time, and when the drovers hit their bed-rolls he warned them to be ready for an extra early start.

It was a starlight night without a moon and in the stillness the night-riders could be heard crooning quietly to the tired herd. The drovers, weary after the long day in the saddle, were soon asleep but Wes who could not rest until all the horses were well cared for was last to get between his blankets. He always slept near the remuda and was in the semi-sleep stage when he heard a slight movement. Instantly he was awake but he did not move. Suddenly he realized someone was approaching the horses. His eyes strained, piercing the darkness. A black shape moved to the picket line, and threw a saddle on to a horse. Wes was about to get up to help when he remembered Wade's words. He lay still and watched. Having saddled his horse the man unhitched it and moved slowly away from the picket line.

Wes slipped from his blanket and, watching the shadowy outline carefully, he crept stealthily to his horse. He soothed the animal with a soft word and quietly saddled the horse, all the time keeping an eye on the man who was becoming lost in the darkness. When he was satisfied, Wes unhitched the horse and led it with a stealth which matched that of the man who had left camp. He quickened his pace until the outline of the man became visible and then he matched step for step.

Wes knew he must be careful, he must not be seen, for he felt as if he was close to discovering something important. If this man was on legitimate business why leave the camp in such a manner? Wes knew he must find out who the man was and where he was going.

About half a mile from the camp the man mounted his horse and rode at a walking pace until he reckoned he was out of earshot of the camp. When he put his horse into a long steady lope Wes was relieved. The slowness of the action was getting him down but now with the movement, he felt he had a chance to take his bearings. Wes soon realized that they were heading for the herd trailing behind them!

CHAPTER EIGHT

They had travelled about four miles when Wes saw a gleam of light ahead and very shortly realized it was a camp fire. He pulled to a halt and listened. As well as the pound of the hoofs ahead, he heard the unmistakable sound of cattle. A low moan of a herd some distance to his right drifted to him. The man must be making for the camp and this was Lunt's camp. Wes' brain pounded. Why was one of Jed's men visiting Lunt? Whatever happened he must find out and he must do it without being discovered.

He sent his horse forward but soon slowed his pace. The night was wrought with dangers to him and he must not betray his presence. To ride straight ahead would be to court disaster. Wes veered to the left and was pleased when he saw a rise in the ground loom up. He sent his mind back trying to remember the terrain which they had passed through earlier that day. Excitement seized him when he recalled that the rise constituted a long, low hill which stretched for about three miles.

Wes swung round the side of the hill until it shielded him from the camp. He increased his pace in order to shorten the distance which the unknown rider had gained.

Twice Wes halted, slipped from the saddle and crept to the top of the rise to take his bearings. At his third halt he found he was as near to the camp as he dare ride. He secured his horse and, after surveying as much of the ground as he could in the darkness, he slid quickly over the top of the hill and made his way speedily but quietly in the direction of the camp.

What cover there was was small but Wes made good use of it and was able to get close to the camp. From the black outlines he deduced that most of the men were asleep but two stood close to the fire whilst a third held a horse near the chuck wagon. Wes tried hard to identify the man from where he was but he realized he would have to get closer in order to be able to be certain. He could hear the murmur of their voices but even though they carried on the still night air they were not distinct enough to make out the words.

Wes moved from behind the low shrub he was using as cover and crept quickly to a small cluster of rocks. Still he could not make out the men. About five yards ahead and slightly to his right was another cluster of rocks. He would be dangerously close to the camp and they would not provide the adequate cover he would like. However, Wes realized he would have to take the risk if he was to identify the men and hear some of their conversation.

As he moved, his foot scraped against a rock. Wes froze to the ground, willing it to open and hide him. The conversation stopped. Wes felt naked. The two men must be staring in his direction; they must see him. The urge to jump up and run was great but Wes fought against it. He dare not move his head to see what was happening. The seconds seemed interminable. Any moment he expected to hear a footstep near him and a voice command him to stand up.

The voice spoke. 'It's only some animal.'

Relief swept across Wes as the second man answered and the conversation continued. He raised his head slowly and, seeing all was as it had been before he scraped the rock, he crept forward to the cover of the low rocks. One of the men half turned and Wes recognized Carl Lunt. If only he could identify the other man. Wes strained his ears hoping to catch the man's name in the conversation.

'There must be no slip up this time.' It was Lunt's voice. 'It means a lot to me to get those ranches. I thought I had it sewn up when I got rid of Matt Gort then along comes this Jed Masters to get those humbugs out of a jam.'

'I've done my best, boss, but jest can't bring that herd to a stop. When Jed Masters gits his mind set he takes a bit of holdin'.' The speaker kept his voice low, and although he could make out the words Wes could not recognize the speaker from his voice. His mind raced with what he had discovered. From those few words Carl Lunt admitted being behind Matt Gort's death and it had been done in order to ruin the small ranchers around Crystal City. Since the herd had got on the trail Lunt had been behind all the misfortunes and attempts to stop it getting through. Wes' mind was so preoccupied with his thoughts that he nearly missed the next piece of the conversation.

'...and if anything goes wrong I still hev one idea up my sleeve but I'd rather you took care of things at the Red River.'

'I'll do that, boss,' came the reply. 'I reckon I'd better be gettin' back.'

'Did you fix things so you wouldn't be

missed?' asked Lunt.

'My bed-roll will need close inspection to see I'm not there.'

'Good,' laughed Lunt.

The two men started to walk towards the horse and in doing so the man's face showed momentarily to Wes. Shorty Jones! Wes almost spoke the word aloud in his excitement. His brain was reeling. When the men reached the horse Wes was galvanized into action – he must beat Jones back to camp.

Wes turned and crept quickly away from his cover and when he reckoned it was safe enough to get to his feet he ran with a crouching gait to his horse. He unfastened it, flung himself into the saddle and turned the animal away from the top of the rise. He was anxious to get moving but he knew undue haste now, whilst still fairly near the camp, could prove his undoing. He kept the horse to a steady pace until he reckoned he could dispense with caution.

The horse responded instantly to his call for speed and in a matter of moments the animal was at full stretch with the ground flashing beneath the flying hoofs. Once he broke from the protective cover of the hill, Wes kept to the straight track and only deviated when the light of the camp-fire came into sight. He was hoping by this course to outride Shorty Jones without discovery.

The noise of the fast moving horse woke some of the men and Jed and Wade were running to the remuda as Wes pulled the animal to a halt and quickly surveyed the horses. Shorty Jones' mount was not there! He had beaten him back!

'What's goin' on? Where hev you been Wes?' demanded Jed. Whilst there was annoyance at not being consulted about Wes' absence there was also a touch of curiosity in his voice. He felt that Wes could not have been absent without good reason and Jed sensed an urgency about his appearance and manner.

Wes ignored the question and threw the reins to Wade. 'Quick, fasten him behind the chuck wagon, out of sight,' he said. Wade was astonished but there was an urgent authority about Wes' voice which made Wade obey without query. Wes turned to Jed. 'Shorty Jones' bed roll quick,' he said and started across the camp.

Jed was beside him in an instant. 'What's goin' on?' he demanded.

'In a minute, Jed,' replied Wes.

They reached Shorty's bed roll. The man appeared to be still sleeping. Wes bent down

120

and pulled back the blanket. Jed gasped when he saw no one there. 'What...?' he started but Wes silenced him.

'Tell the men to get back under the blankets. They must appear to be asleep,' he instructed.

As Jed issued the order Wes replaced the blanket.

'Come on,' he added. 'We'll join Wade over by the chuck wagon.' When they reached the chuck wagon Wes told them quickly what had happened.

Excitement seized both Jed and Wade as they listened to the story in silence.

'Good work, Wes,' praised Jed when Wes finished. 'Now, we know Carl Lunt is behind everythin'. He wants to stop this herd gettin' through in order to ruin the small ranchers around Crystal City, grab their land at a cheap price an' build up a cattle empire.'

All conversation ceased when Wade signalled to be quiet. A faint sound drifted to them and the three men watched intently. A few moments later a shadowy form emerged from the darkness. It assumed the shape of man and horse. The man fastened his horse to the picket rope and was in the process of unsaddling when Jed, closely followed by Wade and Wes stepped forward. Jed's hand hovered close to the butt of his Colt.

Shorty Jones was startled by the footsteps behind him and, when he swung round, his eyes widened with surprise at the sight of the three men. He had come into the camp quietly and everyone appeared to be asleep. These men must have been waiting for him, but how had they known? He glanced quickly across at his bedroll. It did not look as though it had been disturbed. Something was wrong. Shorty was on his guard. His mind became ice-cool, feeling himself cornered.

'Where hev you been?' asked Jed tersely.

Shorty's mind raced. He felt from Jed's tone that the trail boss already knew the answer to that question, and if that was so, it could mean an end to Carl Lunt's ambitions even though he had said he had some other plan in mind. Shorty felt he had been dogged by ill-luck in his efforts to carry out Lunt's instructions, and now all he saw was one chance left to him. He eyed the three men in front of him, two men and a youngster as he saw them. The odds were against him but he would take the chance, maybe he wouldn't delay the herd completely but if he destroyed the driving force behind it he may gain time for Lunt. Shorty realized he must seize the right moment and he must play a delaying game until that moment arrived. With his mind made up he felt himself go tense inside but he was alert.

'Well?' demanded Jed annoyed at Shorty's hesitancy.

'Been ridin',' explained Shorty. 'Thought I heard trouble out there.'

Jed's eyes narrowed. Shorty was being vague and evasive. 'If you heard trouble you should hev woken me,' snapped Jed. 'You know thet.'

'Wal, I wasn't certain, we'd had a hard day an' I figured it was no use waking you if I was mistaken.'

'Quit stallin', Shorty,' Jed's voice relayed his disbelief and contempt. 'We've examined your bedroll, deliberately made up to give the appearance you were still in it. Besides you were followed. You've been working for Lunt an' I reckon most of the troubles we've hed hev been caused by you!' Jed saw his words stinging Shorty.

The drover's eyes narrowed. He did not speak for a moment as he weighed up the situation. 'If you'll let me explain...' he started.

'Explain!' shouted Jed. 'You'll not explain; you'll tell me everythin' an' thet's the only way you'll git off lightly.'

Shortly smiled coldly and seemed to relax. In that moment he was at his most dangerous. He gave his opposers a sense of false security in which their vigilance slackened. Shorty's hand snaked like lightning to his holster and swept upwards bringing his Colt clear of the leather in one movement. His finger was squeezing the trigger as the bullet hit him. As quick as Shorty had been Jed had detected his first movement and his reaction was so fast that his Colt cleared leather that vital fraction of a second sooner than Shorty's.

Shorty staggered under the impact and his aim was destroyed. The bullet nicked Jed on the fleshy part of his upper arm. Jed fired again and Shorty's knees buckled. As he pitched to the ground Shorty tried desperately to line his Colt up on Jed but he failed and lead dug harmlessly into the ground. Jed turned to find Wade, gun in hand, crouching close to the ground ready whilst Wes was laid on the ground, incredulous at the speed of Jed's draw. Jed pushed his Colt back into its holster as Wade straightened and Wes scrambled to his feet.

The camp was alive, as drovers leaped from their beds and ran to see what had happened. Jed soon had the excitement subdued and two men were detailed to bury Shorty.

'Will you go fer Lunt now?' asked Wade when coffee had been poured.

'I'd hoped fer more information from Shorty but he was a loyal follower to the last, prepared to try to get me even when cornered,' replied Jed. 'I reckon I could call Lunt out on what Wes heard,' he went on, 'but right now this herd is more important.'

'But thet will leave Lunt to hit back,' protested Wade.

'Once he learns that Shorty is dead he'll figure we might know somethin' an' therefore might play things cautious fer a while,' commented Jed. 'I hope he does because I'm stickin' with this herd through to Sedalia now. Once that is safely delivered an' I hev the cash for those ranchers then I'll deal with Lunt.'

CHAPTER NINE

In spite of the disturbed night, Jed had the herd on the move before daylight. Things were going to be tough when they reached the Red River. Once they smelt the water after days without it, the steers would take some controlling. Jed had issued his orders clearly to his men so that each one knew precisely what was expected of him. Charlie was dispatched to find a ford which he could use to get the chuck wagon across the Red River and as the wagon rolled away Jed did not expect to see it again until darkness.

Wes took his remuda to the front of the herd, hoping that his pace would help to regulate that of the following cattle. The herd was kept strung out and little pressure was exerted from behind, the drag men concentrating on keeping the stragglers from falling too far behind. As the sun and the heat began once more to make itself felt men's mouths and tongues dried out and became swollen. Every man knowing the nearness of the river was tempted to break away and gallop for the water but they remained, concentrating their minds on the cattle, knowing that once they got the smell of the water they would have their work cut out to prevent the steers from piling and trampling each other in their desire for the water.

As they drew near the river Jed watched the lead steers carefully. Suddenly a big steer lifted its head. He had got the smell. Jed stood in his stirrups and signalled to Wes who let the horses have a little more head. Other drovers saw Jed's signal and passed it on until the drag men knew that already the front of the herd would be breaking into a run. At first it was feeble, the strain of the days travelling without water making itself felt, but gradually as the certainty of nearby water grew stronger the run became faster. Gradually the faint breeze carried the smell back through the whole herd and the run became a thundering earth-tearing gallop. Drovers spurred their horses, riding this way and that, wheeling and turning, shouting and cajoling through their parched lips in their efforts to keep the herd strung out, to avoid the killing bunching as they went into the water.

As the run became faster Wes let the horses go but he kept close to them to keep them moving far out into the water once they reached the river. Suddenly it was there, the swirling waters of the Red River, cool, inviting, after days of dry travel. The horses needed no persuasion to enter the water, and as Wes glanced back he saw the lead steers breast the top of the bank and race down the gentle slope towards the river.

Dust rose skywards from the thundering hoofs in a great choking cloud. Cowboys fought for some measure of control as the following cattle poured after the leaders sending them half way across the Red River before they could get something of a drink. Jed was everywhere, telling the drovers to encourage the cattle to splay out along the river bank so that they did not pile up in one awful jam causing numerous drownings. Men were dispatched to force the leaders onward to the far bank of the Red River there to let them have their full of both water and grass.

Throughout the whole morning the drovers worked unceasingly to get the herd safely across the wide river and not until it was certain that every longhorn was across did they relax and enjoy the water themselves.

Cattle were spread over a wide area on the

north bank of the Red River but Jed did not worry. The herd was safe and it was refreshed and renewed with life to continue the trail to Sedalia. During the afternoon Jed did not press the men too hard for now there was a new feeling amongst them and Jed sensed it. The dissensions and grumblings caused by Shorty's subtle suggestions were gone, once more they were a team, working together fully. In this renewed feeling Jed knew they would win through to Sedalia.

He might not have felt so happy and confident about the future if he had known that the whole morning's happenings had been watched by Carl Lunt from a hillock some distance upstream. Lunt watched with interest the natural confusion which reigned from the moment the herd broke into a gallop for the river. With cattle piling into the water the moment was ripe for Shorty Jones to put their plan into operation but nothing happened. Lunt was puzzled and as time dragged on it became obvious to him that something was wrong something had happened to upset their plans. The added confusion he had planned which would have meant the loss of the greater part of the herd was not forthcoming and, as he saw the herd reach the far bank of the Red River safely, an angry Carl Lunt turned his horse to ride back to his herd determined that he would see to his final idea himself, that plan he would not entrust to anyone else.

Both men and animals seemed to find a new vigour on the north bank of the Red River and the herd under Jed's authority made good progress throughout the succeeding days. Still suspicious of Carl Lunt, Jed left a man behind at the Red River to report on Lunt's actions. Lunt's herd too had suffered in the travel through dry lands and things got out of hand at the water. The trouble plus the fact that he had a larger herd caused delay and a whole day was spent before the cattle were across. Lunt's movements were watched over the next few days as both herds moved northwards but he made no attempt to interfere with Jed's progress. When Shorty did not report and when they found the grave Lunt guessed Shorty had run into trouble.

Jed found that his herd was moving faster than Lunt's and that gradually he was increasing the distance between them. A buoyant mood swept through the men and, as the days passed and Lunt made no attempt to impede their progress, Jed began to forget him, thinking it possible that Lunt had accepted defeat. But one thing Jed did not forget – one day he would bring Lunt before the law for the murder of Matt Gort.

So the herd progressed northwards. Monotonous days of travel were broken by the occasional stampede of frightened cattle, and the extra work of fording streams and rivers. Weeks went by and when Pete reported they were within two days drive of Sedalia relief and excitement flowed through the drovers. A new bite came into their work and they pressed the steers into more speed.

It was late afternoon when Jed called a halt half a mile from the pens at the railhead outside Sedalia.

'We can't hold the men in camp all night,' he commented to Wade. 'Jest keep sufficient for night ridin' the herd an' let the rest into town but warn them I'll expect them to be fit to take the cattle right in tomorrow morning. I'll pay them part of their wages now.'

Wade acknowledged the order and, after the herd was bedded down, he issued his instructions to the drovers. Before long shouting, gesticulating cowboys were running for their horses. The end of the trail always brought its excitement and, released from the tensions and monotony of the long drive, it was only natural that the high spirits of these men should overflow. The loneliness of the trail was past, new faces were to be seen and feminine company awaited in Sedalia. In a few minutes, yelling and shouting they thundered away from the camp.

Jed watched them go with a smile and he tried to find Wade. He saw Wes hurrying towards him.

'Hi, not goin' into town, Wes?' asked Jed surprised that the youngster had not ridden off with the other men.

'I'll ride with you if you don't mind, Jed,' replied Wes.

'Sure,' answered Jed. 'But there'll be little excitement, Wade and I are goin' to close the deal on these cattle; we must be ready to bring them in to the pens in the morning.'

'I'd still like to be with you,' answered Wes.

'Right, see that the horses are ready,' Jed smiled as Wes hurried away. In a way he was rather pleased that Wes had chosen not to ride into town with the others. This had been his first drive and the excitement attached to the town at the end of the trail must have been tempting. He knew Wes was grateful to him for bringing him on the drive and Jed felt that he had found a companion for future trails wherever they took him.

Jed heard the sound of an approaching horse and he turned to see Wade riding in from the herd. With the lines his thoughts were taking, he suddenly realized when he saw Wade how close they had become on this drive. They had worked more as partners than as trail-boss and ramrod and he knew he was going to miss Wade once they broke up after the herd had been sold.

So it was that Jed brought up the subject of the future as they rode to the rail-head. 'Where are you headin' for when we finish here, Wade?' he asked.

Wade shrugged his shoulders. 'Not given it any thought,' he replied. 'Maybe I'll drift back to Texas an' join another drive.'

'How about you, Wes?' asked Jed with a grin.

'Don't know,' replied Wes. 'But I'd like to make sure Carl Lunt pays for what he did to Matt Gort.'

'Then you're goin' to have to stick with me,' said Jed.

Wes' face brightened at the knowledge that Jed had not forgotten what had happened to his friend.

Wade glanced at Jed. 'You better count me in too.'

Jed smiled. 'Right, an' after we've settled with Lunt maybe we should head for Texas together and pick up another herd.'

'Suits me,' grinned Wade.

'And me,' added Wes, delighted that he had been accepted as an equal into a partnership with these two men.

As they neared the rail pens the noise of bellowing cattle greeted them and Wes, seeing a rail-head for the first time was overawed by the sight. Cattle were herded together in fenced enclosures and empty ones were being filled by drovers who had just arrived with the herd. Dust rose everywhere, men shouted and yelled quirting obstinate steers, forcing them out of the corrals into the cattle trucks drawn close alongside the pens. Everywhere there seemed to be pandemonium but to the more experienced eyes of Jed and Wade it was the organized upheaval of the rail-head when longhorns were being shipped.

Several cowboys were sitting on one of the corral fences and Jed, recognizing one of them, turned his animal in that direction. Wade and Wes followed him. A smile broke across the cowboy when he recognized Jed.

'Hi, Jed,' he welcomed as Jed pulled his horse to a halt in front of him. 'Didn't know

135

you were a Sedalia man.'

'First time,' replied Jed. 'Brought a herd up from southern Texas fer a number of small ranchers. How's prices?'

'Good,' replied the cowboy. 'Good job you've got in now; I can see prices tumblin'. There's a lot of cattle being pushed in here. I reckon it will be hard on herds comin' in later.'

'I'd better git them sold,' said Jed smiling to himself at the thought that Carl Lunt might get lower prices. 'Where are the buyers?'

'Martin Richards, over there is the only one left buyin',' replied the cowboy, indicating a smartly turned out man who was surveying the steers, which were being penned, with a critical eye. 'He'll drive a hard bargain.'

'Thanks,' said Jed. 'Probably see you later.'

He turned his horse and, with Wade and Wes beside him, rode over to see Martin Richards. He was a dark man with long side winders running low down to his jaw. A thin moustache added a suave touch to the slim man whom Jed reckoned to be in his early thirties. His blue shirt was held at the neck by a thin black tie and his smart fawn trousers were neatly tucked into the top of black riding boots. A pearl handled gun hung low from his waist. Jed reckoned him to be tough, in spite of his debonair appearance. No man would survive a cattle town unless he was.

'Mister Richards?' said Jed pulling his horse to a halt.

The man surveyed the three riders casually before his eyes settled on Jed and he acknowledged Jed's query. Jed swung from the saddle and extended his hand which he found taken in a firm grip.

'I'm Jed Masters, this is Wade Evans and Wes.' The men exchanged greetings then Jed went on. 'I've three thousand head of cattle half a mile out. Brought them up from Crystal City, they're in good shape.'

Richards nodded. 'And you're lookin' for a buyer.' He smiled. 'I'll buy them but my price is five dollars a head.'

'What!' Jed gasped with astonishment at this low offer. This price would be no good to the ranchers back in Crystal City. 'But I thought longhorns were bringin' a good price.'

'They were,' agreed Richards, 'but there are so many, the market price is droppin'! To tell you the truth I don't really want them but I'll take them off your hands.'

'I can't sell at that price, you must be jokin'.' Jed still couldn't believe the seriousness of the offer.

'Sorry, I wish I were,' replied Richards. 'We never expected so many steers comin' in. I've still got five thousand down the trail that I bought from Carl Lunt yesterday.'

'Carl Lunt!' Jed was astounded. He exchanged glances with Wade who was equally surprised by this news. So this was why Lunt had been quiet since the crossing of the Red River. He must have found out that cattle were flooding into Sedalia and that prices would drop and certainly his five thousand herd pushed on to a heavily supplied market would send prices dropping. He must have outridden Jed's herd and sold before Jed's arrival. 'You should deal with herds as they arrive; Carl Lunt's is back some way.'

Richard's eyes narrowed. Jed could feel him bristling, annoyed that someone should be telling him what he should do.

'I can please myself who I deal with. No one tells me what to do,' he snapped.

'I hev a number of small ranchers around Crystal City depending on me to bring them a good price; it's a question of survival to them,' protested Jed.

'Thet doesn't interest me,' replied Richards tersely. 'I'm not here to give charity; this is big business with me. Lunt arrived

138

and offered his cattle at a dollar a head less than I was paying at the time. I've dealt with Lunt before so I trust him, his cattle hev always been in good condition. I'd hev been a fool to throw away his offer. Naturally his offer lowered my price to others and since then more cattle hev come in. I'm sorry but you should hev got here sooner. Now thet's my offer, take it or leave it.' He eyed Jed for a moment waiting for him to speak but when no answer was forthcoming he turned and leaned against the fence to examine some cattle in the corral.

Jed knew from Richard's action that he had said his last word on price and that it was no use arguing with him. Jed was fuming at the thought that Carl Lunt had out-witted him and it looked as though he had won in his effort to bring the small ranchers into a position where they would have to sell.'

'Wal, Lunt's had the last laugh,' he said dejectedly when he joined Wade. 'Where do we go from here?'

'Wonder if we can find another buyer,' suggested Wade, 'if we were lucky enough to do so his prices would not be much higher, with Richards quoting prices so low.'

Whilst they were discussing their next

move a young Army officer, smartly turned out, hurried towards Richards.

'Richards,' he said loudly, when he reached the corral fence. 'I'm buying three thousand head of cattle, the price is nine dollars.' Richards turned to the fair haired officer. 'I can let...'

'There's one condition,' cut in the officer. 'The cattle are needed urgently at Fort Riley, and I want every possible minute used to get them there. They must be moving before dark.'

'Now, lieutenant, I have the cattle,' replied Richards, 'but I can't get them on the move before the mornin'; I've got to hire the men to drive them.'

'Hire then now,' said the lieutenant.

'It isn't as easy as that,' answered Richards. 'But I'll have them by the morning.'

Wade glanced down at Jed and saw that the same thought had struck him. 'Thet price is good,' he said quietly. 'The ranchers should be all right with it.'

Jed stepped forward. 'I hev three thousand cattle you can hev at that price,' he said.

The officer looked surprised at the interruption. He eyed Jed up and down. Richards' face clouded with anger.

'The offer was made to me,' he snapped.

'You keep out of it.'

The lieutenant glanced sharply at Richards. 'Anyone can take up my offer if they can fulfil the conditions,' he said tersely. He turned to Jed. 'Can you get the herd moving today?'

'They're bedded down half a mile away,' replied Jed. 'We can hev them movin' in no time.'

'Right' said the officer. 'You've got yourself a sale. If you'll come with me we'll sign the necessary papers and I'll give you details about delivery of the cattle.'

As he turned to walk away, Jed fell in beside him, leaving behind a fuming Martin Richards, annoyed at having lost a nice profit. Wade and Wes leading Jed's mount, followed on horseback both delighted at the sudden switch in their fortunes.

When the lieutenant collected his horse they rode into town to the hotel where the officer had taken a room for his buying visit to Sedalia. Here the contracts were signed and instructions given to Jed.

'Present that contract at Fort Riley when you deliver the cattle and you will be paid,' said the lieutenant when he handed over the paper.

'It's a longish drive,' commented Jed.

'I know but as a compensation I am authorized to pay you an extra dollar per head for every steer safely delivered.'

'Fair enough,' said Jed. 'But tell me, why is your price reasonable when Richards was quoting low?'

The lieutenant smiled. 'I've known Richards for quite a while. He's a shrewd business-man and drives a hard bargain; his one trouble is that he tries to buy on the cheap at times; mind you there are a lot of cattle in Sedalia at the moment. Now I'm not in a position to barter, if I were I'd save the Army some money, but the price is fixed by the authorities and there's no more I can do about it.'

Jed nodded, thanked the man and left the officer's room to join Wade and Wes who had waited in the lobby for him.

'Wes, get back to the herd as quickly as possible an' tell the men still there to get ready to move the herd. We're takin' it to Fort Riley.'

'What!' The information brought a gasp of surprise from Wade. 'Thet's a rough, tough drive from here.'

'Sure is,' agreed Jed, 'but it was thet or accept Richards' offer which would have been ruinous to the ranchers. On your way, Wes.'

The two men watched the youngster swing on to his horse and head out of Sedalia for the herd. 'We'll hev to round up the men,' added Jed.

'They aren't goin' to like it,' said Wade.

'I reckon not, but maybe a bonus will persuade them,' answered Jed.

The two men stepped from the sidewalk and hurried across the dusty street towards the End of the Trail Saloon knowing that was where they would find most of the drovers.

CHAPTER TEN

The noise from the saloon met the two men before they reached the batwings. Shouts and laughter and the noise of constant conversation almost drowning the plaintive notes of a piano which reached their ears as they stepped into the building.

Jed took in the scene in one sweeping glance. The saloon was packed with drovers enjoying their release from trail driving. The long counter was crammed with men calling for drinks, the tables were all occupied by drovers and saloon girls. Whilst the gambling tables were in full swing easing from the drovers their end of trail pay. Many of them would return south broke, money gone on girls, gambling and drink. But they would come north again with another herd.

Jed and Wade started to move amongst the tables, threading their way towards the bar. Wade was the first to spot two of their men. They were sitting at a corner table with two saloon girls for company. Wade went to them.

The men glanced up as he stopped at their table. 'Hi, ramrod,' slurred one of them.

'Hooray for our ramrod,' shouted the other.

They all laughed and the girls gave out a cheer.

'I want you two outside,' said Wade. His serious face jolted the two men. Their smiles vanished.

'What's wrong, ramrod? Cheer up,' said the first one.

'We're hitting the trail again, so on your feet an' outside,' said Wade.

'What!' both men gasped together. They exchanged amazed glances.

'I aren't goin',' slurred one.

'Nor me. I've done my ridin' an' I've got me a little girl,' said the other. He grinned and kissed the painted lips of his girl.

'We haven't delivered the herd yet,' rapped Wade.

The two men looked contemptuously at Wade and turned their attention back to the two girls.

Suddenly Wade leaned forward and grabbed the nearest man by the shirt front and jerked him upright out of his chair. He pulled the astonished man round and pushed him in the direction of the batwings.

'On your way,' he rapped.

The man swung round, annoyance on his face at this treatment. He lunged at Wade but in his state he was not quick enough and Wade's fist took him on the point of the jaw. The man staggered backwards, crashed against a table scattering the contents and the occupants, and slumped to the floor.

Wade swung round quickly to see the second man springing to his feet and clawing for his gun. Wade's hand moved like lightning and the drover found himself facing the cold muzzle of a Colt before his own had cleared its leather.

'Leave it!' rapped Wade.

The man hesitated for a moment then let his gun slip back into its holster.

Wade indicated the man on the floor. 'Pick him up an' take him outside.'

Reluctantly the drover shuffled round the table and, grasping the man under the arms, dragged him unceremoniously outside.

A silence had descended on the saloon and Jed took advantage of it. 'Any men in here who trailed with me I want them outside,' he shouted.

A murmuring broke out and heads were turned as several cowboys made for the batwings. As Jed and Wade crossed the saloon the normal everyday noise was resumed and the incident almost forgotten.

When they stepped on to the sidewalk they found all their drovers who had come into town waiting for them. The man whom Wade had hit was just recovering.

'I'm sorry about this,' apologized Jed. 'But we've got to take the herd on to Fort Riley an' we've got to move now.'

The grim faces which showed annoyance at being turned out of the saloon were provoked into reflecting anger. Protestations arose from the drovers.

'We've just got into Sedalia.'

'Thought we were only comin' this far.'

'You were goin' to sell the herd here, what's happened?'

Angry murmurings went round the drovers. One man stepped forward. 'We agreed to bring a herd to Sedalia; we've done that. I say it's not up to us to go any further. I want the rest of my pay an' I'm signin' off,' he yelled.

A roar of assent came from the other men. Jed understood their feelings. They had reached the end of the drive as they thought. A day spent getting the cattle into the pens at the railhead and they would be free with plenty of money in their pockets. A good time awaited them in Sedalia and now he was telling them there was more trail to be faced. He was asking them to spend days in the saddle, to eat and breathe dust again, dust which had become so much a part of their lives throughout the past days but which they detested. Jed sympathized with them.

'I'll give anyone his pay who wants it,' said Jed. 'You'll hev to come back to the herd now because I'm movin' on. But hear me out first. I can't get a good price here, if I take what they're offerin' it would mean ruination for the ranchers we're representin'. I hev had a better price offered by the Army but I've got to take the herd to Fort Riley. I know you signed on to bring the herd to Sedalia, wal, so did I but I'm not goin' to let those ranchers, back in Texas, down. You know that I believe the trouble we've hed on this drive stems from Carl Lunt, wal, I believe he wants those ranchers ruined so's he can get their land cheap. I want to see he doesn't get it. Now git your horses an' we'll head for the herd, those of you who want their money can hev it but they'll miss the good bonus I'm offerin' when that herd reaches Fort Riley.'

Jed and Wade stepped off the sidewalk and

swung into their saddles. As they galloped down the main street the drovers hurried to their mounts and were soon falling in behind their trail-boss and ramrod. Jed hoped the ride back to the herd would give the men time to think favourably about his words and his hopes were fulfilled when, on reaching the herd, not one man asked for his money. Some of them apologized for being awkward when first told about the extra miles to be covered.

They found that Charlie had the chuckwagon all ready to move and Wes had prepared the remuda for further travel. The riders who had been left with the herd were all prepared to move again and, when the men from town joined them, the herd was soon heading in the direction of Fort Riley.

Four days later when Carl Lunt rode into Sedalia he ordered his men to drive the herd straight to the railhead pens whilst he sought out Martin Richards. He found him in the saloon and greeted him amiably, ordering drinks for them both.

'The steers are being put into the pens now,' Lunt informed Richards. 'I'd like to get the transaction settled as soon as possible so I can get back to Texas an' buy out some ranchers who are holdin' back on my expansion. Everythin' go right when Jed Masters came in?' he asked.

'It was,' Richards replied, a partial apology in his tone.

Lunt looked at him sharply. 'What do you mean?'

'Wal, I offered a low price an' gave him perfectly good reasons why it was low. He was goin' to have to take it or be stuck with his herd.'

'Get on, get on, what happened?' snapped Lunt irritably, sensing his scheme had come adrift.

Richards stiffened. 'Now hold on,' he rapped sharply. 'I'm under no obligation to you. I was doin' you a favour.'

'In return for lettin' you hev my cattle for a dollar a head cheaper,' Lunt reminded him. 'However never mind that.' His tone was quieter. 'What happened?'

'The Army stepped in with a better price,' Richards replied and went on to tell Lunt what had happened.

Lunt cursed at the luck which seemed to go along with Jed Masters. All his attempts to delay or destroy the herd had come to nothing and now Masters seemed to have won through. It was a thoughtful Carl Lunt who rode back to the herd and, by the time he reached it, he realized he still had a chance to see his schemes come to a final fruition in his favour.

He took his foreman Blackie to one side and explained the situation to him. 'I'm headin' for Texas right away,' he went on. 'If I can persuade the ranchers that Jed Masters has double crossed them and isn't comin' back they'll sell out to me. This added drive will delay Masters but it would be better still if he was delayed permanently.' He smiled as he saw Blackie grin his understanding. 'And to make doubly certain that no one else can carry the job through, the herd had better be scattered; it's rough, tough country thet it's passin' through and a scattered herd will mean big losses.'

'Leave it to me, boss,' said Blackie. 'I'll brief the boys an' after a couple of nights in town they'll sure be ready for some sport.'

Carl Lunt left for Texas the following morning feeling sure in his mind that he could not fail this time.

Jed soon found that the drive to Fort Riley was going to be a hard one. The terrain was rough and grass was sparse and before long he realized how essential the cattle were to the Army for itself and the Indians under its supervision. Once they were away from

Sedalia the drovers soon forgot their disappointment and threw themselves wholeheartedly into the task of getting the steers to Fort Riley. They found the bonds built up on the trail to Sedalia strong enough to overcome the disagreements there had been. The added incentive of extra money also helped to ease the strain of the added drive.

The drive went well for a week. There had been problems especially over a particularly narrow and rocky section of the trail. It slowed their progress but the drovers worked hard to overcome the difficult terrain and Jed was pleased that they lost only six longhorns.

It was as they broke camp and got the herd on the move on the seventh day out from Sedalia that Jed first felt ill at ease. He could not put his finger on anything in particular but the feeling persisted throughout the day. He kept it to himself, not even mentioning it to Wade. It would, in all probability, turn out to be nothing and he did not want to cause any alarm. They were moving along a fairly wide valley and Jed got the feeling they were being watched. He kept a sharp look-out all day but, when he saw no one, he put the feeling down to the added strain after the long, trying trail to Sedalia. Now for the first time he was wanting the drive over and have the herd off his hands. As he rolled himself in his blankets that night he hoped that he would feel better after a good night's sleep.

Jed found himself waking several times during the night and the following morning he still had the same feeling of being watched. They were in Indian country and, although the Army officer had assured him that there was no danger from the tribes Jed was beginning to have his doubts. Before they broke camp that morning Jed took Wade and Pete to one side.

'I want you to keep this to yourselves, but all day yesterday I had a feeling of being watched and I hev the same feeling now. Hev either of you experienced it?'

Both men shook their heads. 'You're worryin' about getting this herd through,' suggested Wade. 'Take things a bit easier an' you'll be all right.'

'Maybe so,' mused Jed thoughtfully. He glanced at his scout. 'Pete, you haven't seen any unusual signs?'

Pete shook his head. 'Nothin' to cause alarm.'

'Don't roam too far this mornin',' ordered

Jed, 'an' report in at mid-day.'

As Pete hurried away to collect his horse from Wes, Jed turned to Wade. 'Keep movin' around the herd today an' keep a sharp lookout.'

'Right, Jed,' said Wade, 'but I think you're imagining things. Sure you don't want me to warn the men?'

'No,' replied Jed. 'We'll keep this to ourselves but if anything suspicious crops up then we'll take action.'

Drovers were already mounting their horses when Jed and Wade reached the picket-line. Wes had saddled their horses and soon the drovers were bringing the herd to readiness for its daily travel. Shouting and yelling the men brought the reluctant steers to their feet and, with each man taking up his position, the herd got on the move. Throughout the morning everything went smoothly and Jed began to dismiss his ill-feeling but he anxiously awaited Pete's report. As he rode towards the chuck-wagon about mid-day he saw Wade riding in.

'Everythin' quiet,' grinned Wade as he swung from the saddle hoping his boss had got over the anxiety which he had been feeling.

Jed nodded but glanced along the valley

155

for sight of Pete. Jed and Wade had almost finished their meal when the sound of approaching horse brought them to their feet. Wes ran to take Pete's horse as he dropped from the saddle and strode to Jed and Wade. He noted the anxious look on Jed's face as he awaited the report.

'Haven't seen a sign of anyone all morning,' reassured Pete, coming straight to the point. He could sense the relief which Jed felt.

'Good, I reckon I must hev got over tired,' said Jed. 'Guess you're ready for some of Charlie's grub.'

'I am,' smiled Pete, 'but I must tell you that we face two very rough days travelling; the country is rough and is a mass of small hills and valleys.' He collected a plate of stew from Charlie and rejoined Jed and Wade. 'Any particular orders for this afternoon?' he asked.

'When will we hit this rough country?' Jed queried.

'Late afternoon,' replied Pete. 'I'd bed the herd down just this side of it then I reckon you need spend only one night in it.'

'Right, we'll do that,' agreed Jed. 'Find a suitable place to bed down an' search out the best way through the rough country.'

Pete nodded and Jed and Wade returned to the herd which was still moving steadily westwards. As soon as he had finished his meal Pete rode ahead of the herd ranging the countryside in the lonely life of a trail scout.

It was mid-afternoon when Pete found an adequate place for the herd to bed down. The site was at the edge of the hills and Pete reckoned he had time to scout into them for a short way, so that he would be able to advise Jed on the route he should take. He had ridden about five miles and was descending a steep slope into a narrow valley when by chance he glanced upwards. Pete was so startled to see a man, rifle in hand, at the top of the hill that he seemed to freeze to the saddle momentarily. The man's rifle was at his shoulder and even as Pete started to fling himself from the saddle the bullet took him in the head pitching him lifeless to the ground.

The man lowered his rifle slowly, his eyes intent on watching the scout for signs of life. He made his way slowly down the slope keeping the still form covered with his rifle and it was not until he stood over Pete, and saw that he was dead, that he relaxed. Pete's horse startled by the sudden crack of the rifle, had stomped a short distance away and the man hurried to it. He picked up the reins and led it back up the slope where he mounted his own horse and rode away with both animals.

The sun was lowering when Jed recognized rougher terrain ahead. He was puzzled. It was time they were starting to bed down the herd but there was no sign of Pete. Jed was anxious, for it was not like his scout to leave them so long without news of a suitable place to spend the night. If Pete did not arrive shortly they would have to bed down where they were. The same thoughts had struck Wade and a few moments later he galloped over to join Jed.

'What are we doin' boss?' he asked as he pulled alongside Jed. 'It's gettin' late.'

'I know,' answered Jed. 'I expected Pete to be back by now.'

'Wonder what's keepin' him,' said Wade. 'We can't give him much longer than five minutes.'

'Right,' agreed Jed. 'If he doesn't show up we'll bed down where we are. I don't like it much, too confined and too rough,' he added glancing round the shallow valley along which they were travelling towards the hills.

The two men rode on in silence and Jed found the uneasy feeling returning to him. He sensed eyes peering from the rise on either side of them. He was almost glad when Wade informed him that the five minutes were up for now there would be more activity. They searched the distance around them and, seeing no sign of Pete, decided to call a halt.

In the ensuing work of settling the herd Jed forgot his uneasy feeling and when he finally rode into camp for the evening meal his only anxiety was for Pete. He voiced his thoughts to Wade.

'Wal, he's stayed away before,' replied Wade.

'I know, but not when I told him specifically to be back,' said Jed.

'He must hev a good reason,' answered Wade. 'Maybe he's run into difficulty tryin' to find a way through the hills.'

'Could be,' agreed Jed.

Drovers were not long out of their blankets once they had finished their meal, and they were soon asleep.

It was around midnight when the sound of a hard ridden horse woke the camp. Jed grabbed his holster and scrambled to his feet, gun in hand. Wade was beside him in an instant.

'Someone ridin' fast,' he whispered.

'Sure are,' replied Jed. 'Comin' from the direction of the herd. Smells like trouble.'

A form loomed out of the darkness and a few moments later the rider was hauling his horse to a sliding halt. Alarm seized Jed when he saw it was one of the night-riders. He slipped his Colt back into its holster which he was holding in his left hand, and stepped forward to meet the man who was leaping from the saddle.

'What's wrong?' asked Jed seeing the alarm on the man's face as the light from the flickering fire fell upon it.

'Carlos an' Red hev been knifed!' he panted.

There was an involuntary gasp from all the drovers as they caught his words. Automatically they moved forward closing around Jed and the rider.

'What!' Jed was shocked by the unexpected. 'Knifed?' He was incredulous. 'What happened?'

'Don't know,' replied the drover. 'Mike an' I were circlin' the herd an' came across them face downward, knife wounds in the back.'

'Indians?' queried Jed.

'No.' The man shook his head. 'Couldn't be, no scalps were taken, besides there were boot marks around the two bodies.'

'You sure?' asked Jed.

The man nodded. 'It was not good to see, but I'm sure.'

Jed was puzzled and looked at Wade but he could offer no explanation. 'Could this be tied up with Pete's non-appearance?' he queried, voicing the question which had flashed into Jed's mind.

'I hope not,' replied Jed. 'You'd better double the night riders for the rest of the night an' put a guard on the camp, then we'll ride out and take a look.'

Wade issued his orders quickly and, before long, he and Jed were riding for the herd. They learned nothing more than the drover had told them and, after questioning the other night riders, all of whom had heard nothing, they returned to the camp.

'Seems you could have been right about someone watchin' us,' conceded Wade as they sipped a cup of coffee which Charlie had prepared whilst they had been away.

'Then somebody's trailin' us,' said Jed. 'But who and why?' He was puzzled by the whole affair.

'Any connection with Carl Lunt?' suggested Wade.

'Can't see that,' said Jed.

'He could hev heard what happened in Sedalia an' knowin' we were goin' to get the money required by the small ranchers, has put someone after us to stop us.'

'Wal, I suppose that's possible,' agreed Jed. 'Or it could even be Martin Richards – he was annoyed when we stepped in with our herd on offer to that lieutenant. But one thing, we're goin' to get through.'

CHAPTER ELEVEN

There was no more sleep for the drovers that night and, before they broke camp early the following morning, Jed briefed them all to be extra careful, to keep an extra lookout and to report anything unusual immediately.

They found the going very rough and troublesome throughout the morning and progress was slow but much to Jed's relief nothing unusual occurred.

It was shortly before mid-day that one of the point men rode back to report buzzards circling a short distance ahead.

'I don't like the look of this,' commented Jed as he and Wade put their horses into a gallop.

They had to bear to the right and after topping a rise they found themselves on the edge of a steep decline leading to a narrow valley. They pulled their horses to a halt and scanned the slope.

'Over there!' called Wade, pointing down the slope to his left.

Both men swung out of their saddles and scrambled quickly down the side of the hill sending soil and stones tumbling in front of them. They did not speak when they stopped beside the body and saw it was Pete but the glances which they exchanged spoke volumes.

They carried Pete to the top of the hill and Wade rode back to the chuck-wagon for some spades. They buried Pete in the lonely hills as the herd trailed past pushed onwards by drovers now nervous by the three murders. Disquiet surrounded them; they grew fidgety, and to some extent, afraid of the unknown which was stalking them. If they could have seen or known who had perpetrated those acts they would have faced the future with less apprehension. Jed and Wade tried to instil some measure of confidence back into them and, after the herd was bedded down for that night, Jed called all the men together.

'I believe that we have been shadowed most of the way from Sedalia,' he told them. 'I can't be certain who it is but I'm goin' to work on the theory that it is a continuation of Lunt's efforts to stop us sellin' this herd. He started with the murder of Matt Gort an' now is prepared to murder again. I figure the three killings are a prelude to something bigger, maybe an' all out attack on the herd. The killings were intended to get us all jittery, but I want them to have the opposite effect; I want you all to be extra alert especially tonight. If anythin' else is to happen it will follow quickly after the killings – this is ideal country in which to scatter the herd if you want the losses to be heavy an' cause a big delay; but we're goin' to be ready for the killers. I know you are all tired so we'll sleep in turns but the instant anythin' happens if it does, I want immediate action so sleep with your guns on and your rifles handy.'

The drovers who settled down for the night were weary men, but they were men alerted by a determination to avenge the deaths of the riders, who had been their close companions over many miles of trail.

Apart from the usual night riders Jed had positioned men around the herd, but at points further away, so that an earlier warning would give the drovers more time to act. There was still some light in the western sky, giving that half light before darkness in which imaginations can run wild. When the shot came it was some considerable distance to the left of the herd, and immediately the night riders closed in on the cattle quietening their restlessness. The drovers in the camp did not waste a second and were soon swinging on to their horses which had been left saddled. Jed with Wade close behind him led the thunderous gallop in the direction of the shot.

Several more shots followed as drovers out on patrol closed towards the same area. Riders loomed out of the gathering darkness and, as Jed saw several of them heading for the herd, he turned his men across their path. Flashes split the darkening countryside and black forms broke in two as riders were tumbled from their horses by blazing lead. Jed wheeled his horse as a rider flashed behind him towards the herd. His Colt crashed and Jed saw the man reel in the saddle and fall to the ground.

The noise, although not too close to the herd, disturbed the longhorns and a restless wave moved through them. Drovers moved quickly calming them, keeping them from breaking away. Jed saw Wade and two drovers gallop past him in the direction of the herd. He was thankful that Wade had already sized up the situation and was taking more help to the night-riders with the herd.

More firing broke out away to Jed's left

and he spurred his horse in that direction. Suddenly a horse loomed out of the darkness. The rider wheeled and bore down on Jed who was almost taken by surprise. There was a great roar close behind him and he saw the man jerk in the saddle. His horse shied and the rider was flung to the ground. Jed hauled on the reins checking the gallop and turned his horse to see who had saved his life. A horse almost crashed into him as the rider pulled the animal round sharply and Jed had a glimpse of Wes as he came between him and the man on the ground. A Colt roared and Jed saw Wes lurch, but his right arm came round and he squeezed the trigger of his Colt before he slumped sideways and fell from the saddle. The man on the ground crashed backwards as Wes' bullet took him in the heart. Jed, alarmed when he saw Wes was hit, was out of the saddle before his horse had stopped. He fell on his knees beside Wes and relief swept over him when he saw Wes grin at him.

'You all right?' asked Jed.

'Shoulder hurts,' said Wes struggling to sit up. Jed saw that the bullet had taken Wes high on the shoulder but the wound was not serious.

'You'll be all right, once Charlie's had a

look at it,' said Jed.

'Guess I should learn to stay on a horse,' smiled Wes wryly as he got to his feet. 'Thanks for savin' my life, Wes,' said Jed. He felt the words were inadequate but he knew Wes would know his true feelings. 'Let's see who it is – might give us a clue as to what's going on.' They stepped over to the body.

'Blackie Fitch!' gasped Wes.

'You know him?' said Jed with surprise.

'Sure,' replied Wes turning to Jed. 'He's Carl Lunt's foreman!'

'So Lunt is behind these killings an' this attack,' mused Jed. 'He's still determined to stop us selling this herd. Wal, Carl Lunt has something to pay fer when I git back to Sedalia. Guess he'll be takin' a break there. Come on Wes we'll get you back to Charlie.'

As they mounted their horses and started for the camp Jed realized that the firing had stopped. He could distinguish the pound of hoofs fading into the distance, above the bellowing of the disturbed cattle. He was thankful that the thunderous sound of a stampede was absent and he knew that the added help provided by Wade had been effective in keeping the longhorns quiet.

Charlie soon attended to Wes and apart from feeling stiff and sore he was none the worse. Drovers who had spread across the country-side in their pursuit of the riders began to return in ones and twos. Jed was relieved to find that they had lost only one man. Several of them had been wounded but none seriously. Wade rode in to report that all was well with the herd.

Jed called all the men around him and after praising them for their action went on to tell them about Blackie. 'Once again we have mastered Carl Lunt's efforts to stop this herd. I don't think there will be any more attempts but you never can tell. We have only two more days drive and this will really be the end of the trail.'

By the time they bedded down the herd the following day they were through with the rough country and they began the long gentle slope away from the hills towards Fort Riley.

The next day the fort was in sight and Jed and Wade rode ahead to make arrangements to hand over the herd as soon as possible.

'We're mighty grateful for these cattle,' said the Army Commander when Jed produced his credentials. 'The Indian tribes are in great need of them and I can tell you every man under my command will be pleased to see you,' said the officer as he took Jed and Wade to the quarters which would be at the disposal of the drovers. 'Guess your men will be glad to be at the end of the drive.'

'They sure will,' agreed Jed. 'I'll pay them off once we've handed over the herd; how long any of them will stay I don't know but Wade, myself and one other will be leavin' as soon as possible tomorrow.' Jed noted the look of surprise on the officer's face. 'I expect you thought we'd like a few days break but we hev some unfinished business which needs attending to as soon as possible.'

'In that case,' said the Commander, 'I'll arrange for payment to be made today then you needn't be held up at all tomorrow.'

'Thanks a lot,' said Jed. 'That's mighty kind of you. I reckon we'd better git back to the herd.'

'Mind if I ride with you?' requested the officer.

'Not at all,' replied Jed.

The three men were soon heading for the herd at a steady lope and when they reached it the officer eyed the cattle with an expert eye. He remarked about their good condition, and when Jed commented on his knowledge, the officer told him he was preparing for the day when he left the army and had a small ranch of his own.

The men who were to handle the cattle for the Army were waiting at the corrals which had been erected. Everything went smoothly and once the last longhorn was in the corrals the drovers rode into the army post and Jed reported to the Commander. The tally of steers was brought to the officer and the payment was made immediately.

Jed went to the quarters set aside for the drovers where he paid the men their dues plus the bonus he had promised them. He thanked them for their support throughout the long drive.

'If you're likely to drive again next season, we'd be mighty pleased to ride with you,' said one of the men and there was a murmur of agreement.

'I'm mighty grateful you feel like that,' said Jed. 'My plans aren't made but if you're down Crystal City way we might meet up again. But first I've got to see Carl Lunt.'

The following morning Jed, Wade and Wes left Fort Riley after fitting themselves out with supplies to see them as far as Sedalia. They kept to a pace which was not too tiring for themselves nor for their horses but which was fast enough to get them there quickly.

It was late afternoon when they rode into

Sedalia and booked in at the hotel.

'Got a man by the name of Lunt stayin' here?' asked Jed as the clerk showed them to their rooms.

The man looked thoughtful for a moment then shook his head. 'No,' he said. 'Can't recall the name at all.'

After they had cleaned up, the three friends made their way to the cafe. Jed was alert, his eyes missing no one. He was here for a purpose and he was determined not to let Lunt see him first.

'I guess Carl Lunt will get a shock when he sees us especially as he will be expectin' Blackie Fitch,' remarked Wade during their meal.

'You're sure he'll still be in town?' queried Wes.

'Wal I guess so,' replied Jed. 'He must hev put Blackie after us, surely he would await his return, then he would know if his way was clear to get at the   all ranchers.'

'Funny he wasn't known at the hotel,' said Wade.

'There are a couple of other places he could hev stayed,' pointed out Jed.

When they had finished their meal they continued their inquiries but the results were negative. Jed was puzzled, it began to appear as if Carl Lunt had never been in Sedalia.

'Let's make inquiries round the saloon,' he suggested.

Again they drew a blank. 'What now?' asked Wade as they stood beside the long mahogany counter.

Jed looked thoughtful. 'There's one man might be able to help us,' he remarked. 'Martin Richards bought cattle from Lunt, maybe he would know, especially if he worked with Lunt over the offer for our cattle.'

'It's certainly worth a try,' agreed Wade.

Jed called the barman over. 'Know Martin Richards?' he asked.

'Sure,' came the reply. 'Who doesn't in Sedalia?'

'Know where we can find him?'

'Sure, on the north bound stage,' answered the barman. 'Left about ten minutes ago.'

'Thanks,' said ed somewhat dejectedly, and the barman ved away to serve another customer.

'Wal, I guess that's that,' said Wade.

'It needn't be,' put in Wes. 'The stage can't be far, we could easily catch it and talk to Richards.'

Jed and Wade exchanged glances. 'He's

right,' said Jed. 'C'm on.'

The three men hurried from the saloon to their horses. They left Sedalia by the north road and wasted no time in putting their mounts into a fast gallop.

It was not long before a small billowing cloud of dust marking the progress of the stage became visible when they topped a slight rise. The trail moved in a huge sweep across the scrub-land and Jed turned his horse off the trail so that they would cut across country and head off the coach.

The dust puffed from the earth, torn by the hoofs of the three horses, and billowed in small clouds behind them. After ten minutes hard riding the three men came on to the trail some distance ahead of the coach. They pulled to a halt beside the trail and relaxed in the saddles, recovering from the fast ride. When the stagecoach began to near them, Jed rode out into the middle of the trail and raised his right hand signalling it to stop.

The stage driver and his shotgun had noted the three horsemen cutting across country and kept track of them as the coach moved steadily along the trail northwards. When he saw the three riders halt beside the trail the driver became suspicious as to their intentions although he could see no reason why the stage should be held up, for there was no gold or cash on board.

'Better be ready, jest in case,' he remarked to his shotgun. 'Maybe they don't know we hev nothin' of value this trip.'

The shotgun eased the rifle in his hands and was prepared for instant action. 'Their guns are still in their holsters,' he observed as they neared the three riders. 'An this hombre's holdin' his gun hand up,' he added when Jed moved on to the trail. 'Doesn't look like a hold-up to me.'

The driver grunted still trying to decide whether to put the horses into a fast run or not. As nothing resembled the usual pattern of a hold-up and there was nothing of value on board he decided to be cautious and to halt.

As the stagecoach stopped, Jed greeted the driver and shotgun, who had his rifle lined in Jed's direction, in a friendly manner. 'Hev you a passenger by the name of Martin Richards on board?'

'What if we hev?' replied the driver.

'Jest want a word with him,' said Jed amiably. 'I think he has some information for me.'

There were only three passengers in the

stage and Richards was surprised when he heard his name mentioned. He put his head out of the window to see who was speaking but he did not recognize any of the riders. Curious, he called out, 'I'm Martin Richards, what do you want?'

The three horsemen instinctively turned their horses nearer the coach. Jed smiled. 'Howdy, Richards, remember me?'

Richards puckered his brow. He shook his head. 'Can't say I do.'

'I'd better refresh your memory,' went on Jed. 'You offered me a low price for my herd an' I'd hev had to take it if the Army lieutenant hadn't arrived.'

For a fleeting second Jed thought he detected a look of alarm in Richards' eyes but the cattle dealer recovered his composure almost immediately. 'Of course I remember you now,' he smiled. 'Hope you got your herd delivered safely.'

'We did,' replied Jed. 'Now if you wouldn't mind steppin' out of the coach I'd like a chat with you.'

Richards looked surprised. 'But what about? I don't think...'

'You'll find out in a moment. I don't want any unpleasantness so just step out here.'

'Now see here...' began the stagecoach

driver but he was stopped by Wade who had almost imperceptibly moved his hand close to his gun butt. In a flash the gun left its holster and the driver and shotgun found themselves staring at the cold muzzle of a Colt almost before they realized it.

'Jest keep quiet,' rapped Wade. 'Shotgun jest ease that rifle to the ground an' both of you keep your hands where I can see them.'

There was a moment's hesitation as the shotgun annoyed that he had been caught in spite of his vigilance, weighed up the possibilities of out-manœuvring these men. He realized there wasn't a chance and threw down his gun. Both men raised their arms.

In the meantime as Richards opened the door and climbed out of the coach Wes drew his Colt and moved so that he had the other two occupants covered.

'Wal, what is it?' snapped Richards glaring angrily at Jed who swung out of the saddle.

'Richards,' said Jed looking hard at the man facing him. 'I believe Carl Lunt put you up to offerin' me a low price, you may or may not know why – that doesn't matter – fortunately it didn't come off, now I want to know what happened when Lunt arrived in Sedalia.'

'I don't know what you're talking about,'

said Richards.

'I think you do,' snapped Jed. 'Now answer my question.'

'Wal, nothin' happened,' started Richards. 'He handed over the herd an' I paid him.'

Jed frowned. Richards could be telling the truth. He may have been involved over the low price but not concerned with any of Lunt's other plans. 'Do you know Blackie Fitch?' asked Jed.

'I've heard Lunt mention him as his foreman,' replied Richards.

'Did you know he was sent after my herd to stop it reachin' the Army?' queried Jed.

The surprise in Richards' face struck Jed as being genuine. 'I sure didn't,' said Richards who, realizing that this scheme of Lunt's was bigger than he imagined, went on, 'I only played along with Lunt because he said he'd offer me his herd at a dollar per head less than the marketing price. I couldn't miss a chance like that.'

Jed eyed Richards for a moment. 'All right,' he said. 'I believe you. Now can you tell me where I can find Lunt? I expected him to be in Sedalia awaiting Blackie's return.'

'He left Sedalia for Texas as soon as we'd completed the sale of the cattle,' replied Richards.

Jed was taken aback by the news then suddenly the realization of what Lunt would be doing struck him. The Texan had anticipated Blackie's success in stopping the herd and had returned to Texas immediately to bring his scheme to final fruition.

There was a grim determination as Jed turned to his horse and swung up into the saddle. He steadied the animal. 'Sorry fer stoppin' you,' he called to the driver. 'Hope you all hev a pleasant trip. Wade, Wes, come on we've got a long ride to Texas.'

CHAPTER TWELVE

Carl Lunt covered the miles back to his ranch near Crystal City in quick time, and although he had pushed both himself and his horse hard, a good night's rest, his mind content in the assumption that he would soon have the land he wanted, refreshed him. He knew he would have to move cautiously so as not to arouse suspicion but he started to implement his schemes immediately.

It was a habit of local ranchers to visit Crystal City every Friday and Lunt made it in his way to be in town on the Friday after his return. In the middle of the afternoon Lunt strolled casually into the saloon and, whilst he appeared not to notice, his eyes took in everything as he crossed to the bar. He was aware of the ranchers enjoying a drink together at a couple of tables in one corner of the saloon and he knew that his entrance had attracted their attention. He could almost sense their feelings at his arrival. They knew he had been up the trail to Sedalia with his cattle and that he had left after Jed Masters had pulled out with their cattle. Lunt smiled wryly to himself when he thought how they must be saying amongst themselves. 'If Lunt is back where is Masters with our money?' Before long they would be questioning him.

He proved to be right. In a matter of minutes one of the ranchers pushed himself from his chair and crossed to the bar.

'Howdy, Lunt,' he greeted. 'Bring your drink over an' join us, we'd like to hear how it is up in Sedalia. I'll git you another drink.'

Thanks,' said Lunt, and, when the drinks had been served, the two men crossed the saloon to the tables where greetings were exchanged.

Lunt pulled up a chair. 'How hev things been around here?' he asked.

'Quiet,' replied one of the men, 'especially since the herds pulled out. Did you hev a good trip?'

Lunt nodded. 'Couldn't hev been better, except that prices were low in Sedalia.'

The men looked sharply at Lunt, although they tried to hide their concern. They realized that Lunt knew their position, that they were depending on good prices for their cattle in order to survive.

'How low were they?' queried one rancher trying to sound casual.

'Wal, prices varied. There was a lot of cattle in from all parts, and a lot depended on your time of arrival, prices were droppin' all the time. I was lucky, I got in whilst the prices were not too bad.'

He could see the relief show on the men's faces. If he had got a reasonable price then it followed that Masters must have got one because he had been in front of Lunt on the trail.

'Good, I'm pleased,' replied one of the ranchers. 'We could do with more money comin' into this part of Texas.'

'Wal, if your money comes through as good as mine then you should be all right. Remember, if it doesn't then thet offer of mine fer your spreads can be renewed, maybe at a slightly lower price though.'

'Why shouldn't it come through all right?' queried one man anxiously.

'No special reason,' replied Lunt, 'except that I believe this fellow you hired hed to push on beyond Sedalia.'

'Beyond Sedalia?' The ranchers were surprised at this news.

Lunt nodded. 'I heard tell of a herd that had been bought by the Army, but had to be delivered. It hed been left Sedalia two or three days before I got there.' He paused, but he saw the ranchers were expecting him to go on with some news so he obliged. 'Rumours came in that it had been attacked by Indians and some of the cattle run off.'

Alarm showed on the rancher's faces. 'But I thought the Indians were friendly up there,' said one man.

'They're supposed to be,' replied Lunt, 'but you know how it is when Indians want cattle, they may not wait for the Army and Indian Agency to deal with it. However I shouldn't worry too much they were only rumours goin' round Sedalia, I wouldn't pay too much attention to them.'

Lunt smiled to himself. The seeds of doubt were sown. He wouldn't play it too much now; let them think things over for a while. Worry would be added each day that Jed Masters did not show up and Lunt felt that Jed would now be dead. He pushed himself from his chair.

'Wal, I guess I'd better be goin',' he said. 'It's nice to be back. See you again.' He turned and walked out of the saloon.

Throughout the following week the ranchers spent many anxious moments discussing the possibilities of seeing neither Jed

Masters nor their money. Every time he met any of them Carl Lunt always made sure he asked if they had had any news and he was always able to add to the doubts he had already sown.

Now Lunt began to look out for Blackie's return. As soon as he had Blackie's good news he could really go to work on the ranchers and finally force them to sell out to him. Lunt was making his plans one evening, and was seeing himself as a cattle baron in southern Texas, when the sound of horses brought him to his feet and sent him hurrying outside. In the half light he saw three riders approaching the house but it was a few moments before he was able to recognize them.

Suddenly Lunt stiffened with surprise. They were three of his men but Blackie was not with them. He was puzzled and bewildered as he watched them approach. There was something in their manner which spoke of trouble, of things gone wrong. Greetings were exchanged as they pulled to a halt.

'Where's Blackie?' asked Lunt anxiously.

'Dead,' came the curt reply from one of the men.

'What!' gasped Carl. He was staggered by the reply. This was something that had never been entertained in his mind. Then, realizing they were three weary men who faced him, he ushered them into the house where he offered them all a whisky.

'Wal, what happened?' he asked sharply, wanting to have the story, yet fearing the worst. 'Was the operation a success?'

The three men glanced at each other before one of them spoke. ''Fraid it wasn't, boss,' he said quietly, almost with a touch of apology as if he feared Lunt's reaction.

Carl Lunt scowled; his face darkened and he cursed under his breath. 'What went wrong this time?' he snapped. 'This Jed Masters seems to bear a charmed life.'

The three men went on to relate how they had shadowed the herd and finally attacked it. 'Blackie's idea was to reduce the number of drovers by gettin' some of them on their own and to raise a scare in the others. Seems to me these were the wrong tactics – they certainly put the drovers on their guard,' added one of the men when Lunt was in possession of the facts.

'You could be right,' agreed Lunt.

'They sure were waitin' fer us,' commented one of the other cowboys.

'Do you know what happened after the attack?' asked Lunt.

'We waited in the hills until daylight then we sized up the situation. We found out that we were the only survivors an' so we headed back here.'

'Any of the drovers get killed?' queried Lunt, wondering if Blackie had succeeded in accounting for Masters before he was killed.

'One in the raid but three had been killed before that,' came the reply. 'Masters was gettin' the herd on the move as we watched so I reckon he would get it through all right.'

When the three men left for the bunkhouse Carl Lunt poured himself some whisky, bit on a cheroot and for some time pondered on his position. Jed Masters was sure to return with the cash for the small ranchers and once they had that they would be able to pay off the loans to the bank. His position was hopeless unless he could get the ranchers to sell before Masters returned. Now he realized he had to strike quickly, play on their feelings of doubt about Masters and force a sale before he arrived.

Suddenly, a decision made, he pushed himself from the chair and hurried into the hall. He grabbed his Stetson and left the house. He saddled a horse quickly and in a few moments he was on his way to the

Rocking Chair ranch of John Brady.

Brady was surprised to see Carl Lunt standing on the veranda when he opened the door in answer to the sharp knock.

'Howdy, Lunt,' said Brady. 'What brings you out here at this time of night?'

'I know it's a bit late,' replied Lunt, 'but I figured the news I've just received is important to you and the other ranchers around here. You're my nearest neighbour so naturally I rode round here first.'

Brady was mystified. 'Come in,' he said and stepped aside to allow Lunt to enter the house. When he had closed the door Brady led the way into a room where Mrs Brady was busy sewing. She was equally surprised to see Lunt but greeted him pleasantly.

'I'm sorry to be disturbing you Mrs Brady but I thought it important to see your husband,' said Lunt. He turned to Brady. 'Three of my men just got in from the cattle drive to Sedalia. I did not hurry them back with me; it had been a rough drive and I reckoned they deserved a break. Knowin' the concern of the ranchers fer their cattle entrusted to Jed Masters I inquired if they'd heard any news of him.' He smiled to himself when he saw Brady's intense interest show on his face. 'Apparently the herd was attacked on its way to the Army post.' Shock and fear of the worst revealed themselves in Brady's reaction. 'Masters won through and the cattle were delivered but my men heard that Masters, after paying off his drovers headed north.'

'North!' gasped Brady incredulously. 'But why north?'

'I'm afraid they heard nothin' more than that,' replied Lunt. 'It puzzled me but I thought I'd better let you know right away.'

Brady looked thoughtful. 'Thanks,' he said.

'You don't think Masters has absconded with the money from the sale of the cattle?' suggested Mrs Brady.

'No, surely he wouldn't,' said her husband but his tone indicated he was trying to convince himself as well as his wife.

'But you knew nothing about him when you hired him, John,' she pointed out.

'He was a friend of Matt Gort's, Ella,' said her husband.

'You only had his word for it.'

'But I liked the man,' protested Brady.

'Wal, you never can tell with some of these drifters,' put in Lunt. 'If it is true it will hit some of the ranchers hard.'

'It sure will,' agreed Brady. 'I'm better off

189

than most of them an' I can tell you it will take me all my time to survive. More than likely I'll hev to sell some land to buy cattle an' work on a smaller scale. I feel sorry for the others, they'll be ruined.' He bit his lips hard. 'I reckon some of them will go huntin' Masters an' I'd sure like to join them.' His eyes reflected his desire for revenge on a man who would be regarded as worse than a thief.

'Is there anything we can do tonight?' asked Lunt.

'I guess not' replied Brady. 'It's no good visitin' the others tonight. Let them hev a good night's rest. Plenty of time to deal them the shock tomorrow.'

'It isn't somethin' I fancy doin',' said Lunt, 'will you ride with me?'

'I've a better idea. I'll get word to them all to meet in town tomorrow morning about eleven at the saloon, you be there and we'll break the news to them then.'

Lunt agreed and he left the Rocking Chair ranch highly satisfied with the way things had gone.

The following morning the ranchers were in the saloon when Lunt and Brady walked in.

'What's this all about John?'

'Why the mystery?'

'Something wrong?'

The questions flew as Brady and Lunt joined them.

'Can we use the back room, Charlie?' called Brady to the barman.

'Sure, help yourselves,' came the reply.

Brady and Lunt crossed the saloon followed by the puzzled ranchers.

When they were all assembled Brady called for silence and added, 'Carl came to see me last night with some bad news for us an' I figured you should all meet here to hear it.'

All eyes turned on Lunt who told the ranchers the same story he had told Brady. Immediately murmurings broke out. Everyone was talking at once; pandemonium reigned for a few moments until Brady managed to quieten them.

'Has anyone any suggestions?' he called.

'I'd like to string Masters up,' called one of the ranchers.

'Thet'd be too good fer him,' shouted another. 'He wants something slow and hard.'

Unanimous agreement came from the gathering.

'Hold on,' shouted Brady. 'That may be what he deserves if this is true but remember we hev no proof as yet.'

'I figure he should hev been back by now,' someone shouted.

'Yeah, Lunt's men are back.' Another rancher agreed.

'Don't forgit he had an extra drive,' said Brady, 'an' thet would delay him.'

'Did your men say why he headed north?' queried one of the ranchers of Lunt.

'No, they didn't know,' replied Lunt.

'Then this information could be only a rumour?' suggested the rancher.

'It's possible,' agreed Lunt, 'but I...'

'Maybe Masters had a reason fer headin' north,' interrupted another rancher. 'I reckon we should give him chance to report before we condemn him.'

'If he doesn't turn up it matters little whether we condemn him or not,' called out one of the men. 'I'll be ruined.'

A murmur of agreement passed round the room.

'But we can give Masters a few more days to show up.'

'We won't be able to give him long,' shouted a burly man. 'Once the bank hears of this they'll be concerned about the loans they made to us.

'Wal give him a...'

The statement was interrupted by a knock on the door. One of the ranchers opened it and everyone turned to see the bank manager enter the room. Lunt smiled to himself. He had made it his business to make sure that the news reached the bank manager that morning and the official had reacted as Lunt expected he would.

'I'm sorry to interrupt your meeting, gentlemen,' said the bank manager, a small, thin man whose fair hair was well groomed. He was neatly turned out in a fawn frock coat and matching waistcoat, 'but I think this meeting will be of some concern to me. From what I hear there is some doubt about you receiving the money for the cattle you sent to Sedalia. I don't know what you are doing about it but I thought it right to warn you that your loans cannot be extended. I must have repayments by the end of the week.'

This statement brought gasps of surprise and annoyance from the ranchers. Protestations sprang to their lips.

'But that gives us only three days to find the money.'

'We'll all be ruined.'

'I can't possibly raise the cash before then.'

193

'Give us a bit longer.'

The bank manager raised his hands. 'I'm sorry, gentlemen, I wish I could be more helpful but you must realize my position with so much money at stake. I really do hope you can find a solution.'

Amidst cries of disgust the bank manager left the room and, when the door closed behind him, near pandemonium broke out once again.

Suddenly a voice called out above the others. 'Lunt, Brady, where do you two stand in this? You've the two biggest spreads round here.'

'I'm in almost as bad a fix as any of you. I will hev to sell most of the ranch an' operate on a small scale if I want to stay here. I've given the matter a lot of thought last night an' I figure that doesn't suit me so it will be a question of sellin' everythin' like the rest of you.'

All eyes turned on Lunt when Brady finished speaking.

'Wal, I'm not affected by the none return of Masters so I expect your question means can I help you out of the difficulty?' called out Lunt. 'I'm sorry, gentlemen, I just haven't got that sort of money to lay out in loans.' A faint murmur ran round the group of men. 'I only wish I had,' continued Lunt smoothly. The ranchers were in the situation which he wanted. 'There is one thing I can do though; whilst I haven't the money to lend I would use it to buy your land.'

The ranchers looked at each other talking loudly, discussing the proposition. Whilst none of them wanted to part with their land they realized they were in a situation, the only solution to which seemed to be Lunt's suggestion.

'Wal, gentlemen,' called Lunt to silence them. 'The position boils down to this if you can't pay the bank in cash the bank authorities will take your land in lieu but accept my offer an' you'll be able to pay the bank an' probably still hev some left.'

'Seems the only way,' called one rancher.

There was a murmur of agreement from some of the men whilst some of the others were puzzled by their predicament.

'This seems a fair enough offer by Lunt,' shouted Brady. Lunt smiled to himself. They were talking exactly as he wanted. Before long the land would be his, but his hopes for an immediate conclusion to his plans were dashed when Brady went on. 'But as we have three days in which to find the money I don't see any call for settlin' things now. I'm sure Carl will give us those three days. Who knows, Jed Masters may even turn up.'

Lunt's immediate reaction was one of annoyance. He could make these men sell now by offering a higher price now than he would in three days time but he curbed the words which came to his lips. He hid his feelings for he could not afford to alienate these men and, after Brady's words, he could do nothing but agree to waiting three days.

The ranchers gave their approval and it was arranged that they would meet at eleven in the morning in three days time. Everything was to be ready for a sale if necessary so that the repayment to the bank could be made in the specified time.

As they left the saloon there was not one rancher who had any hope of having the money unless Jed Masters showed up and John Brady hoped his trust in the man had not been misplaced.

CHAPTER THIRTEEN

Throughout the next three days two men were anxious about the arrival of Jed Masters. Carl Lunt, eager for the three days to pass without Jed's appearance, had posted some men in town to report his arrival if he showed up. John Brady did not keep any lookout for the man to whom he had entrusted his cattle. He knew that if Jed arrived in Crystal City he would report to him immediately.

On the morning of the third day Carl Lunt, everything ready for the purchase of the land, rode into town in a buoyant mood. Whilst his schemes had not stopped Jed Masters they had certainly delayed him long enough for Lunt to carry through the deal, forced quickly to its conclusion by his lies. John Brady left his ranch with a heavy heart. This was the last time he would leave the house as its owner.

When Brady reached the saloon he found he was the last to arrive and immediately on his appearance a smile came to Lunt's lips.

'Now, gentlemen,' he said, 'we meet as agreed and, if none of you are able to pay the bank, then I am willing to buy the land from you. My lawyer here will see to the documentation of the deals. I cannot offer you all the same price; as you realize some of you have better land than others but I am prepared to discuss the deal with each of you in turn.'

'Hold on a minute, Lunt,' shouted Brady. 'I'd like to hev one more shot at the bank manager to try to persuade him to give us an extension.'

'I don't think it will be any good,' said Lunt. 'It's only goin' to waste time.'

'I think it's worth a try, it won't take long. What does everyone say?' replied Brady.

The ranchers shouted their agreement. They were willing to clutch at any straw which might enable them to keep their ranches. Although annoyed at the suggested delay Carl Lunt could do nothing but agree. With the hopes of his friends in his hands John Brady hurried from the saloon to the bank.

Half-an-hour later he was back.

'I'm sorry,' he said quietly. 'I could not persuade the bank manager. The money must be repaid today.'

For a moment there was intense silence filled with the disappointment of the men in the room.

'All right,' called Lunt, 'now let's get down to discussion. If you'll all wait in the bar I'll talk to you one at a time.'

The men shuffled from the room and a few moments later the first transaction was being discussed.

Ella Brady straightened from the stove on which she was preparing a meal for her husband's return. The pound of horses reached her ears and she hurried to the window to see who was approaching. Three horsemen were coming towards the ranch at a gallop and Ella gave a gasp of surprise when she recognized Jed Masters. He had returned! Ella's brain pounded with the meaning of it all. If only he had been sooner – now he was too late, the ranch would have been sold.

Ella rushed from the house, and did not await on the veranda for the arrival of the three men but rushed out to meet them.

Jed was puzzled by the fact that Mrs Brady was running to meet them and as they got near to her he saw trouble on her face. The three men pulled to a halt and Jed swung quickly out of the saddle to greet her. Ella gasping for breath almost fell into his arms.

'What is it, Mrs Brady, you look in trouble.'

'The ranchers are selling their land this morning at eleven o'clock,' she panted.

'What!' Jed gasped. 'I thought the money from the sale of the herd...'

'It would have done,' interrupted Ella, 'but we thought you weren't coming back.'

Jed looked puzzled. 'What do you mean?'

Ella quickly told the story of Carl Lunt's visit and the subsequent happenings. The three men listened in amazement.

'We might have known Lunt would work up something,' said Jed glancing at his companions.

It was Ella Brady's turn to be surprised. 'Lunt?' she queried.

'Yes,' said Jed. 'He wants all the land fer himself. We'll tell you about it when we get back, but we must try to stop him. What's the time?'

'It's just gone eleven,' said Ella. 'I've been watching the clock and living every minute with John. I'm afraid you'll be too late.'

'We'll try,' said Jed and swung into the saddle. 'C'm on,' he shouted, and the three men turned their horses and put them into an earth-tearing gallop towards Crystal City.

They did not spare their mounts in order

to reach the town quickly, and heads turned as the three men thundered up the main street. Jed was out of the saddle before his horse had stopped. He leaped on to the sidewalk and Wade and Wes were close on his heels as he burst through the batwings into the saloon. Their sudden impact into the room caused everyone to swing round to see who had come in in such a manner.

For a brief moment the ranchers felt they were unable to believe their eyes. Then as Jed strode towards them, his eyes sweeping the room for Carl Lunt, they all started to call their greetings. Huge grins covered their faces and Jed knew that he was not too late. John Brady was the first to reach him, grasping him by the hand and saying how pleased they were to see him.

'Has anyone sold any land yet?' asked Jed anxiously.

'No,' said Brady.' The first man is in with Lunt now, I'll stop him.'

Jed grabbed him by the arm. 'Hold it,' he said, 'I hev some reckonin' to do with Lunt.'

Brady looked hard at Jed. 'What do you mean?' he asked.

'You'll learn soon enough,' replied Jed. 'Thank goodness your wife knew about this deal and where you would be.'

'An' thank goodness I delayed the proceedings by seein' the bank manager.'

Jed said no more but strode to the door leading to the back room. He flung the door wide open to see the rancher about to sign a paper. The three men in the room stared incredulously at the man in the doorway.

'Masters!' gasped Lunt.

The rancher dropped his pen. 'I am glad to see you,' he called pushing himself out of the chair. Then seeing the look on Jed's face he moved to one side to keep away from the impending trouble.

A weak smile crossed Lunt's face. 'Wal, Masters,' he said, 'I guess there's no need to carry on with our transactions now you've got back.' His voice betrayed his nervousness as he tried to pass off the situation.

'There isn't,' agreed Jed. His voice was cold and bore ill for Lunt, who recognized this fact and knew he was going to have to face this man. 'You've tried all along to ruin the chances of these men savin' their ranches, so that you could buy them. You've coveted them for some time an' saw a chance of ruinin' them when the time came for their cattle to go north.'

'It's not true,' called out Lunt in a plea to the ranchers who were crowded in the doorway. 'Haven't I tried to help you by buyin' your land.'

'And helpin' yourself at the same time so that you could get all the land you wanted,' snapped Jed. 'You tried to prevent the cattle ever leavin' here, first by tryin' to bribe Matt Gort and then by killin' him. You tried the same tactics on me but fortunately didn't succeed.'

'Lies! Lies!' yelled Lunt passionately, revealing the truth in his attitude.

'When you failed here you tried all the way to Sedalia an' there you got the help of Martin Richards,' went on Jed relentlessly. 'Don't look so amazed, Lunt, I've talked to Richards. You forced me to make the extra drive an' put Blackie on me. Fortunately Wes saved my life an' we kept the herd together.'

Lunt licked his dry lips. He saw that the game was up and he must seek an opportunity to get out of his predicament. He feigned a restlessness and started to pace the room as he talked.

'It's not true,' he said. 'You're building up false accusations against me, trying to turn these men against me, why I don't know.'

Jed watched him carefully as he moved across the room talking quickly but even then he was not prepared for the suddenness of his action. Lunt passed behind the lawyer who was still sitting at the table. As soon as the lawyer was blocking Jed's line Lunt pulled his Colt from its holster which almost caught Jed unawares. At the same time he moved like a flash to the window. His finger pressed the trigger but Jed had started to move and the bullet took him in the top of his arm. As Jed hit the floor Lunt flung himself through the window. There was a loud splintering of wood and crash of breaking glass.

Jed was on his feet almost immediately and reached the window before Wade. As he leaped out into the back street he saw Lunt running to the right.

'Stop!' yelled Jed and loosed off a shot at the man.

Lunt took no notice and then as Jed wanting to take him alive gave chase Lunt suddenly turned. The look on his face was like that of a cornered animal. He realized his position was hopeless; he could not get away but he would see that the man who had ruined all his ambitions would die first. His gun blazed but the instant that Lunt had stopped Jed knew what was coming and he was diving to the ground. Pain stabbed through his wounded arm as he hit the hardness. He rolled over and Lunt's bullets went harmlessly wide. Jed squeezed the trigger as his Colt came up on Lunt. The bullet took the rancher high on the shoulder and as he staggered under the impact Jed fired again. He saw Lunt's knees buckle and he pitched into the dust of the back street.

Jed heard feet pounding behind him and as Wade, Colt in hand, ran up to Lunt, Wes and John Brady helped Jed to his feet.

'Are you all right?' asked Wes anxiously.

'Sure,' said Jed. 'It's only a scratch.'

Ranchers who had run from the front of the saloon came racing round the corner and were relieved to find Jed all right. As they crowded around him, Wade reported Lunt was dead.

Jed sighed. 'He's paid fer Matt Gort an' the others.' He paused and looked round the ranchers. 'I guess we'd better get over to the bank and pay a few debts.'

The publishers hope that this book has given you enjoyable reading. Large Print Books are especially designed to be as easy to see and hold as possible. If you wish a complete list of our books please ask at your local library or write directly to:

Dales Large Print Books
Magna House, Long Preston,
Skipton, North Yorkshire.
BD23 4ND

This Large Print Book, for people
who cannot read normal print,
is published under the auspices of

THE ULVERSCROFT FOUNDATION

19

TRAIL TO SEDALIA

n Jed Masters rides into Crystal City, nds a mystery surrounding the death of riend which he is determined to solve. results in him taking over as trail boss herd made up by small ranchers who dependent on its successful sale in lia. Troubles beset him on the trail, and nally sees a connection with an xpected quarter. Proving this is another er, and how Jed does this in the face of accusations make the trail to Sedalia citing ride.